The Hitchhiker

The Troubadour

Two Stories

By

Donald Skiff

© Copyright 2018
All rights reserved.

ISBN-13: 978-1984915238
ISBN-10: 1984915231

Contents

Introduction 4
The Hitchhiker 6
   One 7
   Two 28
   Three 56
   Four 81
   Five 87
Twenty Years On 101
   One 102
   Two 108
   Three 111
   Four 113
The Troubadour 115
   One 116
   Two 125
   Three 130
   Four 138

Introduction

What makes us human? We know that a few other species share with us some of our most valued experiences, such as our ability to perceive and respond to the emotional states of others. Today's technologies remind us of our remarkable ability to deduce even some of the most subtle relationships in our environment, yet much of what we experience is still mysterious to us.

We love to construct grand theories of how things work. Questions, from "the meaning of life" to "does she love me?" occupy our thoughts whenever we lift our heads from the daily grind of survival.

It's often when something changes that we notice the ground that we've been walking on. Our personal narratives, the stories we tell ourselves about ourselves, become disjointed without our being aware of it until an event, or another person, comes along to remind us that we could have done things differently.

Judy Collins, a popular singer from a half-century ago, touched on these questions with two songs about how our perceptions of our personal realities change with time and circumstances.

Both Sides Now[i]

I've looked at clouds (love, life) from both sides now
From win and lose and still somehow
It's life's illusions I recall
I really don't know life at all

Introduction

Send in the Clowns[ii]

Isn't it bliss?
Don't you approve?
One who keeps tearing around,
One who can't move.
Where are the clowns?
Send in the clowns.

"Send in the clowns" refers to the old theatrical device that was used when the script failed—when, as it so often happens in life, we are left to figure out something different.

I invite you to check out the full lyrics of both songs, which even after all these years can stimulate a lot of personal rumination. Better yet, listen to them sung. I'm sure they are available on YouTube.

—Don Skiff, January 2018

Acknowledgments

I am indebted to Marjorie Lynn and Grace Stewart, whose literary critiques were invaluable, and the members of Writers Unlimited, a group dedicated to sharing our writing and our comments and suggestions. And none of this would have been possible without the encouragement and suggestions of my wife, Judith.

The Hitchhiker

One

Walter usually drove the highway with cruise control engaged, but in the gathering dusk he disabled it because he needed to be more alert. There wasn't much traffic on the highway into the city, and he could see an occasional deer. He'd never hit one, although he'd had a couple of close calls. He had thought about getting one of those whistles for his front bumper that are supposed to scare them off, but hadn't gotten around to it.

He lived alone, by preference. Since his divorce six years before, he enjoyed his solitude. He expected to retire from the phone company in another year, and planned to do some traveling after that. In his spare time, he built furniture in his basement, relishing the smell of newly-cut wood and the rich odors of varnish and glue. Most of the finished pieces he gave away to friends.

A car was parked alongside the roadway, showing no lights. He slowed down and gave it extra space as he drove by. As he passed, he saw someone sitting behind the wheel. *Should have his lights on, or his blinkers,* he thought. Glancing in his rear view mirror, he wondered why he would be just sitting there at the side of the road. Maybe he had car trouble.

Pulling off the pavement and stopping, he backed up, watching the other car in his mirror. Within a car's length, he stopped. His backup lights showed a face, but he couldn't tell anything more. He sat there for a moment, wondering what to do—report the car to 9-1-1, and let the police handle it, or get out and at least offer his help. Could be dangerous, approaching a strange car at night on a deserted highway. He turned off the Rachmaninoff that had been playing on his radio.

Getting out and walking back to the parked car, he pulled his phone from his pocket. Because of the darkness, he couldn't see the person clearly, so he switched on the light on his phone.

She looked at him through the glass, terrified.

"Do you need help?" he asked, hoping she could hear him through the closed window. He couldn't blame her for not opening it if she was frightened, but when she didn't answer he repeated his question, louder. She still didn't respond.

He tapped on the glass. "I'm here to help, if you need it," he said, still louder.

She fumbled with the window control, and finally got it open. She still didn't say anything, just looked at him with fear covering her face.

"You should have your lights on, at least, ma'am," he said. "Do you need my help?"

Her voice was soft with apprehension. "I shouldn't be here," she said.

"If you're having car trouble, I can call somebody." He leaned out and looked at her tires. Walking around the car, he inspected the other tires.

"You don't have a flat. Will your car run?" Walter glanced up and down the highway, feeling frustrated. The woman was clearly confused and frightened.

"I shouldn't be here," she repeated.

"Can I give you a lift? I can take you into town if you want."

It dawned on him that she was not functioning very well. Her eyes darted around, at him, at his car, at the dashboard of her car. *Maybe she's had a stroke*, he thought. "I won't hurt you," he said, putting his hand on the door handle.

The Hitchhiker

She didn't seem to react to that, so he opened the car door and extended his hand. "Looks like you might have something wrong with you," he said quietly. "Maybe you had a stroke. Let me take you in to the hospital. Come on, I won't hurt you."

Hesitantly, she gave him her hand, and he led her out of the car and around to the passenger side of his own car. Helping her in, he said, "I'll get your purse and lock your car, okay?"

Securing her car and returning, he got in slowly to avoid frightening her more. In the dim interior light, he smiled at her. "We'll get you some help," he said gently. "Better buckle up."

When she didn't move, he reached across her and fastened her seat belt. All the while, she simply stared at his face, flinching slightly when he touched her, but not making a sound.

Driving on, he thought of looking in her purse to get some identification or a number to call, but decided that it would be safer to wait and let the hospital people do that. He was pretty sure she'd had a stroke, or maybe a mental breakdown. Either way, he needed to hurry and not do anything to upset her more.

She continued to look at him without speaking.

The fifteen-minute ride into town seemed longer. "If you had a stroke, you need medical help as soon as possible," he said.

"I shouldn't be here," she said again.

"Why? Doesn't anybody know where you are? Do you have family or somebody who can come and get you?"

She leaned over and kissed him on the cheek, startling him. She had a slight smile on her face. He glanced at her occasionally as he drove. *Looks like she can move all right. Wouldn't she be lopsided if she had a stroke? She doesn't seem afraid of me anymore.*

"She died," she said suddenly.

Walter looked at her. "What?"

"She died, and I guess it got us mixed up."

The hair stood up on the back of his neck. "Who?"

"I'm not supposed to be here."

He realized that he had been holding his breath. Letting it out suddenly, he slowed the car and looked at her. After a long moment, he said, "I think we have a problem."

She simply smiled at him.

There was nothing to do but continue. Walter felt something approaching panic, but he drove on, hoping that nothing bad would happen in the meantime. He hadn't thought of looking around in her car back there. Maybe she'd killed somebody, and they were stuffed in the back seat or the trunk. Maybe she had a knife in her purse. She hadn't paid any attention when he put it next to her. He glanced at her frequently.

Driving up to the emergency entrance of the hospital, he got out without looking at her and waved at the first person he saw inside. "I found this lady out on the highway. She's not injured that I can tell, but I think she may have had a stroke."

Attendants rushed out with a wheelchair and helped the woman into it. Walter followed after them. "She's confused," he said.

"We'll check her out. Are you her husband?"

"No, I just happened by and stopped. She was just sitting in her car at the side of the road, and she hasn't said two words."

"Could she walk?" One of the attendants took a clipboard from a desk.

"Yes," Walter said. "She doesn't seem lopsided—isn't that a sign of a stroke?"

"Could be. But we'll check. You don't know her, you say?"

"No."

"Would you fill out this form?" The attendant with the clipboard handed it to Walter, while the other one wheeled the woman into triage.

"She has a purse—I'll get it," said Walter, turning toward the door.

When he returned, the woman was lying on a gurney, and people were trying to talk to her. She kept looking at Walter, fear showing on her face. A female doctor looked up at him. "She seems to know you," she said. "Maybe you can get her to speak to us?"

Walter felt committed. He approached the woman and took her hand. "Can you tell the doctors what's wrong?" he asked, feeling inadequate.

By that time she was connected to various machines, and kept looking around at the doctors and nurses, apprehension showing on her face.

"These people are here to help you," Walter said.

"Can you tell us your name?" someone asked.

Walter handed them the woman's purse, which he had been holding. A nurse opened it and withdrew a wallet. "Abigail DeVoe," she said. "Nineteen sixty-four. Lives in Braille."

"A phone?" someone asked.

"No." the nurse continued to rummage through the purse. "No phone numbers, either."

A doctor shook his head. "Why don't people carry identification!"

"Any medical ID?"

"No. One credit card."

"She's had an MI," said a doctor who had been monitoring the woman with a stethoscope. "Sounds okay now, though."

"Get her to the cath lab, stat," ordered another.

"Stay here, please," said a nurse to Walter. He found a nearby chair and sat down.

In a moment, another nurse came to him. "So you don't know this woman?"

"No. I just found her on the highway. She seemed confused. I thought this would be the best place to bring her."

"Good thinking. But we need to find out who she is. Would you object to talking with a policeman?"

Walter sighed. "No," he said, but felt impatient.

In a few minutes, a doctor came out from the treatment area. "She's okay, physically. She's had a serious myocardial infarction—a heart attack—recently, but not a stroke. Maybe a TIA. She'll need to see her regular physician as soon as possible." He smiled. "She's not very talkative."

Walter frowned. "So what are you going to do with her?"

The doctor shrugged. "Let her go. Maybe you can help her get home."

Walter sighed. "Why me?"

The nurse smiled at him. "You're the good Samaritan," she said. "Otherwise, it's the police."

She helped the woman into a wheelchair to take her out to the car. At the curb, the nurse stepped close to Walter and spoke in a low voice, "That resident asshole just wanted to get rid of her. I think she may have had a TGA—Transient Global Amnesia—a kind of amnesia that will clear up in a few hours. It's not usually serious, but she should see her own doctor as soon as possible."

A few minutes later, the two of them sat in his car, still at the entrance to the emergency room. Walter sighed. "Abigail—that's your name?" When she didn't respond, he said, "Your driver's license says you live in Braille. I'll drive you there. Maybe you can connect with your folks. You do have folks there, right?"

Braille was sixty miles away. At the outskirts, Walter pulled into a highway rest area. "I have to use the restroom," he said to the woman, who smiled back at him. "You want to go in, too, or wait out here?"

"I shouldn't—" she began, and he finished it for her: "be here. I know. Okay, just wait here. Don't leave the car."

He hurried into the rest room, suddenly aware that he had been holding his urine for some time.

Back at his car, Abigail sat motionless, other than watching him walk out of the shelter.

"Okay," he said, "I need your address." He reached tentatively for her purse, expecting her to clutch it to her, as most women would. But she still didn't move, simply watching his face with that faint smile on hers.

He pulled her billfold out of the purse, deliberately keeping it and his hands up where she could see them. "One-one-two-one Richmond Street," he read aloud from her driver's license. Turning to the GPS instrument on his dashboard, he entered the address and waited for the confirmation and directions. The female voice visibly startled Abigail. She stared at the instrument.

Walter started the car and pulled out onto the highway. "Now at least we know where we are going," he said. The path to the address was simple, and a few minutes later they pulled up before a large condominium-type building.

"I may need your keys," he said, "in case there's no one else there." He pulled a small key ring from her purse. Besides a key to her car, there were just two other keys. One of them, he decided, must be to her apartment. "Okay, let's go see who you are."

He led her up the stairs to the door to her apartment. He knocked loudly. There was no sound coming from inside. He knocked again; still no response.

"Okay," he said to Abigail, who had meekly followed his lead all the way to the door without any indication that she knew where they were. "We're going in, okay?"

He put the key in the lock and opened the door. "Hello!" he called before entering. The apartment seemed unoccupied. He and Abigail stood just inside the door, looking around at an ordinary apartment. Leading her to a sofa, he gestured to her to sit down, and then explored the rest of the apartment.

As he went, he kept talking to her. "The nurse said you might have had an attack of amnesia, not a stroke. She said it should clear up in an hour or so."

A couple of framed photos stood on top of a spinet-style piano, one showing Abigail alongside a young man, the other showing an elderly couple, evidently taken some decades earlier. On the refrigerator, a note said simply "8:00"

Walter glanced at Abigail, who sat seemingly unaware of where she was. She looked at him occasionally, and smiled. *Doesn't look like she's going to give me any trouble,* he thought, *but she's no help, either.*

"This is obviously where you live," he said to her. "Do you live alone?" To answer his own question, he opened the refrigerator. "Just the food of a woman who lives alone," he said. "A half-eaten casserole of some kind, milk, Coke, tonic water." That prompted him to open the freezer door. Sure enough, a bottle of good gin, along with some store-bought frozen food.

Extracting the gin and a bottle of tonic water, he took two glasses from a kitchen cabinet. "Well," he said to her,

The Hitchhiker

"I need to think." He dispensed ice from the refrigerator door and mixed two drinks. Sitting beside Abigail, he put one drink in front of her and sipped from the other. "You owe me this much," he mumbled, gesturing with his glass.

Looking around the room, he noticed an old wall-mounted phone, and a desk that might reveal something he could use to identify this woman. *The phone won't help, unless the phone number happens to be printed on the dial, the way they used to do. The desk will be the place to start.*

"You're very kind," Abigail said suddenly.

Walter looked at her quickly. "Well, you can speak!"

"You're very kind," she repeated.

"Do you want a drink?" he asked, pointing at her glass and taking another large sip from his. "I sure need one right now."

She looked at the glass sitting before her, but didn't answer. Then she looked at him and smiled.

Abigail was a little younger than Walter. Reasonably attractive, well-groomed graying hair and decent clothing. A skirt, sensible shoes. Her eyes on his pulled at him, but he kept his distance. It had been a long time since he'd felt that about a woman.

"Can you tell me anything about yourself?" he asked. "You said you shouldn't be here—wherever 'here' is. And you said, 'she died.' What does all that mean?"

"I shouldn't be here," she said, pointing to herself. "She died, and I'm here now. I don't know what to do." Her face looked worried.

Walter frowned, then gave a quick laugh, but caught himself. "You mean, you are not Abigail? You're only in her body?" When she nodded, he slumped, his mouth dropping open, and stared at her.

15

"That's why you don't know this place!" He drained his glass. A picture began to form in his mind. He had found her sitting quietly in a car parked at the side of the highway, and the doctors in the E.R. said she had suffered a heart attack. "Abigail what's-her-name had a heart attack on the highway and died," he said. "Then who are you? *What* are you?"

She simply smiled at him.

He reached over and grasped her arm lightly. "Are you some kind of spirit or something?" By this time, he was sweating. "Now, don't tell me you're some kind of zombie. I don't believe in those things. Those are just in the movies."

"I'm here to observe." She spoke as casually as a woman who had just walked into his office. "There was a mistake. I shouldn't be here." She again pointed to her chest.

Walter was speechless for a long moment. "You're kiddin' me, right? You're pretending to be some alien from outer space. Who put you up to this? Charlie and Shep? Those guys have a weird sense of humor, they could do it—but who are *you?*"

"I don't understand much of your language," she said. "I am trying."

He got up and made himself another drink. Standing before her, he managed to say, "You're inside her, but you don't know anything about Abigail?"

"She seems to have some kind of memory, not just before she died, long ago memory. I don't know this place." She gestured around the room. "This was her place?"

He sat down again, at a distance from her. "I guess so. It was on her driver's license." Turning toward her, he asked, "Were you in her when she died? Did you kill her?"

"No. Her life stopped, and I was transferred in. They made a mistake."

"Who made a mistake?" The glass in his hand was shaking, so he put it down on the coffee table.

She shrugged her shoulders.

"Did they kill Abigail?" Walter was having difficulty breathing. "Are they going to kill me?"

"No. They don't do that."

"Well," he breathed out, "I'm sure glad of that. I think."

Neither spoke for several minutes. Walter finished his second gin and tonic. Then he stood up again and faced her. "I don't know what I'm supposed to do! My mind is gone!"

"You are very kind," she said.

He felt that she meant it. Somehow, there was a real person in there, in that dead woman's body. She wasn't some robot or a zombie. She sounded like a real woman. Only she didn't know anything, either. She didn't know what to do. Some alien computer someplace had hit a snag and put her in the wrong body.

"When I first came up to you," he said, "out there on the highway, you looked scared to death. Were you?"

"Yes," she said simply. And then she said, "I was afraid you were going to kill me."

"Why?"

"It's my first assignment. Is that the word? Others said some of you are dangerous."

He scratched his head. "Wait. Wait. You are not Abigail. You're just inhabiting her body. What were you before that?"

She suddenly smiled broadly. "Abigail doesn't have a word for that."

"Oh, shit." He flopped back down on the sofa.

After a few moments of silence, he looked at her. "Then you don't know why she was out there on the highway." He pointed to the refrigerator. "There's a note on the fridge that just says, 'eight o'clock.' I guess that's what it means. You don't know anything about that, either?"

"No."

Another silence.

"She feels something," she said. "I don't know what that is."

"Oboy. That makes two of us." He thought for a while. "Well, here's an idea. Maybe she's hungry. We could do something about that. Or—" and he tried to come up with the words. "If she's now a live human being, or at least part of one, do you know if she needs to use the bathroom?" His face turned scarlet.

"I don't know. She feels something," and she pointed to her abdomen, "here."

"Oh, Christ!" He turned his face away for a moment, then, "Well, if she's hungry, that's easy. Let's try that one."

He took a couple of meals from the freezer, unwrapped them, and put them into the microwave. Then he went back to her. "I'm a terrible nurse," he said. "Sooner or later you're going to need more help than I can give you. I hope eating will do it for now."

"They didn't prepare me for this." She smiled at him.

"Nobody prepared me for this, either!"

When the microwave signaled, Walter retrieved the two meals, set them onto plates and took tableware from a drawer. Sitting beside her on the sofa, he put a plate of food before her. "I hope you know what to do with this." He demonstrated by eating from his own plate.

She copied his motion, put a forkful of food in her mouth, and smiled at him.

"Swallow," he said, again demonstrating.

She mirrored his motion, then put her fork down and lowered her head, smiling. "I'm teasing you," she said quietly.

"Oh, shit!" He flopped back on the sofa. "Now you're making fun of me. *I don't know what to do with you!*"

Still smiling, she said, "Some things are easy. As soon as the food touched my mouth, I knew what to do with it, just from how her body responds." She reached over and touched his hand. "Like this."

He grinned in spite of his tension. "You know, I think Abigail must have been a pretty nice person. You remind me of a robot—do you know 'robot'?"

She thought for a moment, then nodded.

"You remind me of a robot I saw a few months ago. It was a demonstration of programming, and they showed us how every little movement, every gesture, had to be planned and programmed into that robot. But you seem to be able to speak, and move, and even feel, when you didn't know anything about Abigail three hours ago."

"There are parts of her brain that know a lot of things. Only—what happened just before she died—those don't work anymore. She still has some memory, and knowledge about how her body works, and some feelings—" She pointed to her abdomen, "I don't know what that means."

They ate silently. Walter glanced frequently at Abigail, wondering what was going on in her mind and what was going on in the mind of the *whatever it was* that was animating her.

She looked directly at him. "She was called Abigail. Are you called something?"

"Walter."

"You are Walter." After a long silence, "I wish—I wish I were Abigail."

"I guess you are, in a way. You look like her—" He got up and retrieved one of the photos from the piano. Thrusting it before her, he said, "You look just like this."

"Oh, my goodness!"

"But you don't know who this man is next to her?"

"No."

Walter put the photograph back. "I'm guessing that that young man is in for a shock."

She continued to eat the food.

"Your gin and tonic is pretty diluted by now," he said, picking up the glass.

"Is it nutritious?"

He grinned. "Only psychologically."

"You became—looser. Less tense."

He laughed out loud. "I guess I did. I was wound up pretty tight."

"Did it help you think?"

"You know," he said, "you're pretty perceptive. Is that Abigail?"

Smiling, she shook her head slowly. "Maybe."

"Let's try another one, okay?" He went to the refrigerator and mixed another gin and tonic. Handing it to her, he cautioned, "It's pretty strong. It will feel warm in your throat."

Abigail drank the whole thing without pausing.

"Wow," he said, grinning, "how does that feel?"

"As you said, 'warm.' I didn't know what to expect, but it felt familiar."

"She had the bottle in the freezer. People do that when they like to drink it straight."

"Straight?" Then after a thought, she said, "without the water, right?"

"Most people just take little sips." He demonstrated, and she laughed.

Walter sat down next to her. "You know, we still don't know what we're going to do. I don't have a clue, but I don't think I can leave you alone right now."

"You're very kind—Walter."

"Why are you here—there?" He pointed to her forehead. "You just said to observe. What's that mean?"

"I am to spend a time like this—only not here." She pointed to herself.

"How much time?"

She frowned. "I will be in a number of bodies before returning."

Walter took a deep breath and let it out. Then he flopped back against the sofa. Shaking his head, he said, "I don't understand."

"I need to know about you. Not just Walter. All Walters."

"An anthropologist?"

"I don't know that word."

"They do what you're here for, except they don't take over someone's body."

"Humans do that, too?"

"Yes. But—who were you supposed to occupy? You said you shouldn't be there, in Abigail's body. Whose, then?"

"Not a female. Someone who had just died, nearby."

He ran his fingers through his hair. "Have to be someone who just died without great damage to the body."

"Yes."

"Like Abigail, only somebody else."

"Yes."

"I need another drink, but I better not. I have to figure out what we're going to do." He looked steadily at her. "You are a whole lot smarter than I am. What are we supposed to do?"

"They are working on it."

"What? Who?" He sat up suddenly. "How do you know?"

"They've told me."

"Oh, shit!" He collapsed again against the sofa back. "What'd they say?"

"They don't use words, as you do."

"So we just wait?"

She smiled. Abigail smiled. "In our training, we learn how to slow our perceptions down to fit your sense of time."

Walter closed his eyes.

Then the telephone rang.

He hesitated until the phone rang four times. "Hello?"

A man's voice asked, "May I speak with Abigail?"

Walter took a deep breath. "Uh, she can't come to the phone right now. Do you know Abigail?"

The voice hesitated. "Yes. She and I were supposed to meet this evening."

Walter sighed again. "What's your name?"

"Michael. Abigail and I were supposed to meet at eight o'clock, and she hasn't shown up yet. Is she there?" His voice sounded young, and worried. "Is she all right?"

"Uh, do you know where she lives?"

"Yes."

"I think it might be good if you came here."

"What's wrong? Who are you?"

"Please come." Walter waited for a moment, then hung up the receiver.

Abigail was watching him closely as he returned to the sofa.

"I feel like I'm responsible for you," he said, "but I don't know what to do. If this guy knows Abigail, maybe he can at least help me here. *I don't know what to do!*"

Abigail pushed the coffee table away from the sofa. Then she moved over to Walter, lifted her skirt and straddled him. "I know what the feeling is now," she said softly.

His mind spiraled out of control. With practiced hands, Abigail unbuckled his belt and exposed him. Then she readied her own clothing and melted into him and him into her.

Sometime later, they lay entwined and smiled at each other dreamily.

"Was that Abigail?" he asked.

"Only the physical."

"Oh. Oh. That's putting it direct," he said. "Are you— I'm feeling really weird." He pointed at her forehead. "Are you male or female?"

"We don't have that distinction," she said.

"Oh boy." He looked at the ceiling. "I just had sex with an asexual being performing in a dead woman's body."

Abigail smiled. "It was an interesting experience," said the being.

They stood and straightened their clothing. Walter went into the bathroom, feeling almost dizzy. His reflection in the mirror grinned at him.

When he returned, Abigail was seated on the sofa, her hand exploring under her skirt. Walter laughed. "That's like in the movie," he said. "Under the Skin."

She looked at him, perplexed.

"It's about an alien," he said, then stopped. "Oops."

"What's a movie?"

He sat beside her. "I've had a lot to drink," he said with a little laugh. "A movie is a play that is recorded and played back for an audience." He looked at her and laughed again. "I'm not making any sense at all, am I?"

"I'm here to observe," she said matter-of-factly.

"People make up stories about themselves, about others, about events. Someone made up a story about a being from outer space—maybe like you—who puts on a disguise so people think she's human, and then she lures people—men—into a place where their bodies are dissolved into some kind of nutrient for her compatriots. She is catching food for her kind. Does that make sense?"

Abigail made a face. "We don't need that kind of nutrient."

"No, I didn't mean—"

"Are you afraid of me?"

"I'm going to have that other drink," he said, and got up to head for the kitchen.

"Would you make me one, too?"

He turned and looked at this woman with whom he had just made love. *How is it possible?* he thought. *She's playing with me. She's a setup. Charlie and Shep have set me up.* He laughed, and continued to the refrigerator. *Those crazy bastards!*

When he returned, Abigail smiled at him as she took the drink from him and sipped it.

"C'mon," he said. "You're not really an alien, are you? Did Charlie and Shep put you up to this? You've done a really good job, by the way." He drank his gin and tonic to the bottom of the glass.

She looked at him and smiled. "I am trying to understand your words."

"Forget it." Walter wanted to go back and chug directly from the gin bottle until it was empty.

"We coupled," she said seriously. "It was interesting. Do all humans do that?"

"A lot," he said. "Male and female."

She was delighted. 'My goodness!" Pulling her skirt up, she looked down at herself. Then she looked up at him. "Show me."

The Hitchhiker

"You are unbelievable."

"I'm here to observe," she said.

Walter hesitantly dropped his pants to show Abigail—no, the 'being'—what a male human looks like. She—or it—wasn't disappointed.

He quickly put his clothing back together. "You don't have this, where you come from?" he asked.

"No. What's the purpose of this?"

He felt as though she were taking notes. "It's how we procreate," he said.

"The sensations," she said, "were very complex. Does it have to do with why I kissed you, in the car after you had rescued me?"

"Maybe."

"I felt something then—Abigail felt something— that was similar. You were very kind, Walter. She felt drawn to you."

"I guess it's called 'bonding'. What I felt a little while ago, when we made love."

"Love?"

"It's that feeling, when one person is drawn to another—usually of the opposite sex."

"When I said I wish I were Abigail."

"Maybe."

"So interesting."

"How do you procreate?"

"Multiply?"

"Yes."

"We don't."

He looked at her in a new way. "Really?"

"We all come from a single 'song'."

"Song?"

"It's the only word that seems close. The beginning of music."

"You have music?" Walter cocked his head and smiled. Then he picked up her half-finished glass of liquor and drained it. She watched him, amused.

"That's the only way I know how to describe it," she said. "You have music—they told us you do."

"Yes."

"Songs—our version of your songs—spring from individuals, and grow into new individuals."

"Wow." *Like memes,* he thought.

"So," she said, looking at him as she had when she said she wished that she were Abigail, "perhaps that is how we procreate."

"That's beautiful!"

She shrugged. "We haven't had enough songs lately," she said. "That's why I'm here. That's why we are here—to search for songs."

He shook his head. "I don't believe it." Still, he did. Looking at this woman, this very human woman, whose arms around him he had felt just minutes ago, Walter realized that he had been missing something very important in his life, something he glimpsed at this moment. "I wish I could give you a song," he said.

Suddenly overcome, he retreated to the bathroom once more. Without glancing in the mirror, he sat on the commode for a long time.

When he returned, Abigail had gone into the bedroom and was lying on the bed, very still. He lay down next to her. "Are you all right?"

"They have repaired the error," she said softly. "Good bye, Walter."

And that was the end of it, of everything. Of Abigail. Of something that Walter couldn't describe, surely would tell no one, but would never forget. He went into the living room and sat motionless on the sofa.

The Hitchhiker

Sometime later, he opened the door of Abigail's apartment to a stranger, the young man of the photo on the piano. "She's in there," Walter said, pointing. "She died in her sleep."

Walter stayed behind while the young man went into the bedroom and cried over Abigail's lifeless body.

After writing him a note about the location of her car on the highway, Walter let himself out quietly.

Two

Walter, Charlie and Shep sat in a corner booth of The Daily, an off-the-boulevard bar near their office in the telephone company. It was Friday afternoon.

"McKenzie told me today that they're cutting back again the first of the month," Shep said, looking closely at his shot glass that was nearly empty.

"They're always planning to cut back," Walter said.

"We got nothing to worry about," Charlie said, swiveling around to watch the sharp-looking woman who had just entered. "They need us."

The three of them had been friends for seventeen years, when they were all transferred into their department on the same day. Their Friday drink before heading home was a tradition since Walter's divorce, six years ago. They didn't talk about anything important; since none of them were sports fans, their conversations usually centered around work and women. Charlie and Shep were married, and sometimes they envied Walter, whose wife had left him for an airline pilot. Walter had been cynical about women ever since, and the other two men used his experience to justify their own lukewarm dedication to their wives. Friday night was their night.

They'd each had a couple of straight shots. Charlie, in particular, watched the other patrons of the bar as they talked. Walter attended to his drink.

"Y'know," Walter said, "we look around here—and at work, too—at the people and we think everybody is just like us."

"What d'ya mean?" asked Shep.

The Hitchhiker

"Just regular people." Walter finished his drink. "And we never think that, like that guy in the yellow jersey over there, he could be *observing us*."

"So what?" Charlie half stood up, addressing the guy in the jersey. "Hey, here I am, what do you make of this?"

Jersey simply looked away.

Shep laughed. "You're crazy, Charlie. Sit down. You trying to start a fight?"

"No," said Walter, "I mean there are *observers*—just watching us."

Shep looked at Walter seriously. "You mean like the NSA?"

"Who cares about the NSA? No, I don't know, I just—I just think sometimes that there are people—or what we think are people—out there, just *observing us*."

"Whoa," said Shep. "Like aliens from outer space, like in the movies?" He had a disbelieving grin on his face.

Charlie looked at Walter. "Hey, Buddy," he said, "you going ape on us here?"

Walter lifted his empty glass to his lips, as though to distract himself from the subject. Then he got up, picked up his glass and asked, "Anybody else ready for another one?"

Charlie pushed the other two glasses toward him without saying anything. When Walter left the table toward the bar, Charlie looked at Shep. "That's not like him."

"I think our friend needs some soft company," said Shep.

"He's never said anything like that before." Charlie turned to watch Walter across the room. "He was always the one to poo-poo that stuff about alien invasions—or even the idea of other life in the universe."

"Is it paranoia?" asked Shep.

"Sounds like it." Charlie smiled up at Walter, who had returned with their drinks.

"I know you're talking about me," Walter said.

"We're just wondering, Pal," Shep said, smiling.

"I know, it sounds crazy. But—" Walter slid into the booth. The other two waited for him to explain. "I had an experience last week." Walter described his finding a confused woman in her car on the highway, taking her to the E.R. where they said she'd had a heart attack, and taking her to her home in Braille, where she revealed "her" true nature. He didn't mention having sex with her or that she died.

"You think she was just shitting you?" asked Charlie.

Walter grinned. "For a while I was convinced that you two had put her up to it, to string me along."

"How would we know you'd stop on the highway for a stranded motorist?"

"We didn't even know you'd be there at that time," added Shep.

"Yeah, that's what I finally decided." He looked up at the others. "Not that you guys wouldn't ever do anything like that."

They all laughed.

"Then what do you think was going on?" asked Shep.

"She might have been schizoid," said Charlie. "You're lucky she didn't pull a knife on you."

"By the end," Walter said, "she had me pretty convinced. I wanted to get out of there, but if she really had had a heart attack, I couldn't just leave. Then some guy called on her phone, and he evidently knew her, so I asked him to come over. And I left."

"Weird," said Shep.

Charlie looked across the room. "That why you picked out that guy in the yellow jersey? You think he was really watching us?"

"No," said Walter. "Oh, I don't know."
"You're paranoid," said Shep. "She's got you paranoid. I would be, too. That was weird."
"What'd she act like?" asked Charlie, "you just said she acted confused. But when she said she was an alien, she get that bug-eyed look?"
Shep made a face to illustrate the look, and all three laughed.
"No, she acted just like an ordinary woman, but she didn't seem to know a lot of stuff everybody knows."
"Like what?"
"Well, there was a bottle of gin in her freezer."
The others laughed.
"I made up a couple of gin and tonics, cause if she had the stuff she must drink it, you know? But I had to show her how to do it." Walter frowned.
"Whoa," said Shep.
"And how to eat a pot pie that she had in her own freezer."
"You sure it was her place?"
"That's what her driver's license said. And it was her pictures in the apartment."
"Okay," said Charlie, "you have my permission to be paranoid." He looked around. "The guy in the jersey is gone."
All three silently scanned the crowded room.

That evening, Walter sat listening to a Sibelius recording, and thought about Abigail. Then he reminded himself that Abigail was dead. He wondered about the young man who had come to her apartment. Son? Lover? Would he talk if Walter tried to get in touch with him? But she was dead when the guy arrived. How would he even know about the alien? No, he decided, better close that door.

31

But maybe the guy thought that I had something to do with Abigail's death. Maybe right now he's trying to find out who I am. I'd sure be suspicious if I was him.

The next day Walter went to his favorite store, *Lumber and Cabinetry* just to browse through the aisles and inhale the wood smells. There was nothing in particular he needed for his projects, so he flipped through some magazines in the magazine rack.

"Fun, isn't it?" came from beside him.

He turned to see a small woman in work clothes. She was older, he guessed at least sixty, with short straight hair that was going from gray to white at her temples. Her hands were those of a craftsman. (*Craftsperson,* he corrected his unspoken thought.) "I like to just look at how they design things," he said.

"You build?" she asked.

"Yes."

"So do I, when I can get the time," she said. Her voice was husky, almost like a man's.

"What do you like to make?" Walter asked.

"Lots of things. I just like to work with my hands." Her smile seemed vaguely conspiratorial.

He looked around the store. "There's plenty in here to tempt you, isn't there?"

"There is."

Walter put the magazine he'd been holding back in the rack, and turned toward the door. "Good hunting," he said to the woman. He didn't wait for her to respond.

Driving home, he thought about women. *There's all kinds, some good, some like Daniele. That little gray-haired woman I bet you could trust.*

The Hitchhiker

Daniele had been his wife, until she left after twelve years of marriage. She had blindsided him, coming home from a trip to announce that she was leaving him. She'd always been impulsive—charming when she was young, annoying as the years went on. Taking refuge in his basement cabinet shop, he'd questioned whether he should ever have gotten married in the first place.

Back home fixing himself a sandwich for lunch, he thought of the gray-haired woman, wondering what her woodworking projects were like. And then he thought again about Abigail. He realized that he felt a touch of grief for her, especially when he remembered the sex. *That's sick,* he thought. *She wasn't really a woman. What was she? She sure acted like a woman.*

Then he got a phone call from the Braille police. They wanted to talk with him about Abigail. They'd tracked him down from the information he'd given at the E.R.

He offered to go to Braille to talk to them, preferring not to have the police show up at his home or his office. When he got there he told them about finding Abigail and taking her first to the emergency room and then to her apartment, thinking that she would recover from the apparent heart attack.

"I know, it was wrong to just leave," he said, "but I didn't know the young fellow who showed up, and I didn't know what to tell him. I thought I could just disappear."

The officer, attractive in a prim sort of way, smiled wryly. "It looked suspicious, it sure did. But the people at the E.R. said you seemed on the up and up." She looked through her file. "Since the woman had suffered a heart attack in her car, apparently, and then died from another one in her home, there wasn't much to indicate foul play."

The following week, Walter, Charlie and Shep were kept busy, and didn't get together for lunch or Friday drinks. Nothing more was said about Walter's "paranoia."

On Saturday, he made an excuse to go to the wood store. Sure enough, the little gray-haired woman was there, buying plywood. "What's that going to be?" he asked her.

"An old-fashioned dish cupboard."

"With glass doors?"

"Oh, no. Ordinary folks back then didn't have glass except in windows. This'll be painted, with stenciled flowers on the doors. What do you make?"

"I'm working on a desk chair," he said. "Cherry."

"I'd love to see it." There was an impish quality to her, with that conspiratorial smile.

As he watched her selecting a four-by-eight piece of three-quarter inch plywood from the rack, he marveled at her strength, especially since her arms barely spanned the board. "You been at this a long time," he said.

She turned and grinned at him. "All my life. My father taught me cabinet making."

"You inherit his tools, too?"

"You bet." She placed the selected plywood on her cart. You want to see my shop?"

"Yeah. When's a good time?"

"Right now. Lemme check out and you can follow me. It's only six blocks."

Walter felt a giddiness that had not revealed itself in years. Here was somebody who felt the way he did about building things, somebody he might be able to share his interest with. That it was a woman added something he couldn't quite identify. Certainly, she wasn't the kind of woman he'd always known, and there wasn't any sexual energy between them.

The Hitchhiker

Driving behind her pickup truck, he realized that the little feeling he had toward this woman was *safety*. It made him smile.

She lived in a small old house that had a barn instead of a garage—something that had been built a hundred years ago when the neighborhood was at the edge of town, He pulled into the unpaved driveway behind her truck, stopped and went up to the back of her pickup. Lifting the plywood out, he carried it toward the barn, where she was opening the door.

"Thank you," she said, and led him to a large table sitting in the middle of the room. "Right there would be perfect."

The machinery in the barn was all ancient. She'd said that her father had taught her cabinet making, and this had evidently been his shop. Walter identified a large wood-turning lathe, a table saw, a planer and a joiner, and a drill press with a mortiser mounted on it.

"I'm impressed," Walter said.

She wiped her hands on a rag and picked up a small end table, not yet finished. "You said you worked in cherry," she said, holding it out to show him. "Solid cherry."

"Beautiful."

"Old cherry naturally darkens with age, but folks don't want to wait that long these days, so I'm staining it. It's for a friend of mine."

"It tickles me to run into somebody who loves wood as much as I do," Walter said.

She grinned.

"You do this for a living?" Walter asked.

"In a manner of speaking," she answered with a chuckle. "I work with contractors who are building homes."

"I don't know your name," he said.

"Jezebel. Call me Jez."

"I'm Walter. I work for the phone company, but my real work—" He gestured toward the machines, "I don't get paid for." He took out his phone and pulled up some photographs of his cabinet work.

"You give all those away?"

He shrugged. "I just enjoy making them."

"Awesome."

Walter moved toward the door. "Don't want to keep you from your work," he said, "thanks for showing me your shop."

Jez pulled a business card from her pocket. "Gimme a call when you want to chat about wood."

He extracted one of his own cards from his wallet. "Yeah. Same here."

One evening several weeks later, Jez phoned him. "Just wondering if you'd care to have a cup of coffee with me," she said.

He agreed, and put the lid back on a can of wood stain that he'd been stirring. He'd thought of the woman often since they had talked in her wood shop, but Walter had never been very gregarious. He hadn't learned the joys of small talk.

In the Denny's downtown, Jez waved at him rather awkwardly from a booth. Neither of them offered a hand to shake, but simply smiled at each other when he sat down.

"Get your cherry chair finished?" she asked, and laughed at the words. "Cherry-chair."

"Still sanding. My projects take a lot of time. I was just stirring some stain when you called."

"I figured you were the meticulous type."

The Hitchhiker

A waiter interrupted them, and left promptly with their order for coffee.

Jez looked at Walter and pulled her hair behind an ear. "I have a friend," she began, choosing her words carefully, "who asked me to look you up."

Walter looked at her quickly. She wasn't smiling.

"Should I be flattered or worried?" he asked, frowning.

"Probably flattered." She paused, looking directly at him.

After a long moment, she continued, "You met this friend about a month ago."

Walter's curiosity was up, trying to think of someone he might have met. The first one he thought of was Abigail, but he immediately discarded that thought. *She's dead.*

Jez, her face still serious, seemed to be struggling to find her words. "This friend seems to think that you are an open kind of person."

Walter shook his head. "You got me. I don't remember—"

"Yes you do," she said. "You met them out on Route Fifteen, just about dark."

She was watching him carefully.

Walter felt sweat run down his face next to his eye, making him blink.

"See, you do remember."

"Abigail?"

"Bingo. Only Abigail's dead."

Walter shook his head slowly. Chills went down the backs of his arms. "I don't understand."

"Yes you do."

He felt a surge of denial in his throat. "Are you one of them?" he finally asked, his voice breaking on the last word.

"No." Now Jez was smiling. "Oh, hell no." She glanced around the room. "I just have this, uh, *friend* who was there with Abigail last month."

A picture began to form in Walter's mind.

Her voice was a little lower. "You remember when we first met, in the wood store, next to the magazine rack?"

He nodded.

"That wasn't by happenstance," she said.

Walter felt dizzy. He placed both hands on the sides of his head.

"Hey," Jez said, her voice quick with concern. "Ease up, friend. Just relax for a minute. I didn't mean to freak you out."

They sat silently for a long time, their eyes meeting. Walter was breathing heavily. He finally managed to speak, "I was trying to convince myself that that didn't happen."

"I happened to meet them," she said, "pretty much the way you did."

"Them." Walter frowned.

She chuckled. "I don't know how to refer to them. I can't tell if it's one, uh, *person* or if there *are* even individuals."

Walter looked down at his coffee cup. "It did seem to be an individual in Abigail. No gender that I could tell." He thought of how that evening went, of tutoring Abigail, but then of having her suddenly on top of him, tugging at his belt.

"My friend," she said, "has the appearance of a man, younger than you. He has told me that he's not male or female, but it's really hard to keep from thinking of him as *him*." Then suddenly she touched Walter's hand. "You mustn't tell anyone about them."

"You just told me."

"I was asked to. They trust you."

"Why?"

"I don't know," she said. "I guess because of how you were with Abigail."

Walter suddenly felt like crying. "Why me?" He took a deep breath and let it out slowly. He felt something that was like grief, thinking about that woman, how he had taken care of her, not knowing that it was not a *she* at all. For a few hours, he had cared for someone in a way he'd never done before. He couldn't remember his wife ever having been that vulnerable with him. Whatever that *being* was, in Abigail's apartment, Walter felt something for it, an empathy.

He drank the rest of his cold coffee. "What did they tell you about me?" Inside, he was squirming, but he needed to know.

Jez smiled at him. "Everything."

He hid his face in his hands and groaned.

"Understandable, Walter," she said quietly. "You didn't know."

He looked up at the gray-haired woman sitting across the table from him, suddenly feeling a connection. "How did you learn about them?" he asked.

"I was installing some kitchen cabinets in a new house, laying on my back with a screwdriver in my hand, and just shooting the shit with the fellow who was helping me." She grinned widely. "We got to talking about something, and it got to the subject of sex. You know, how guys talk."

Walter grinned back. This was an unusual woman.

"Well, I said that I'd never felt comfortable with sex. I wasn't against it, but I didn't understand what all the fuss was about. And this fellow leaned over so I could see his face through the openings in the cabinet, and he said, 'I don't either.' We both howled."

Walter had to laugh at that.

"Then after we got off work," she said, "we went to a bar for a drink. Well, I'm a cheap date. I can't hold much liquor." She spread her arms out wide. "I ain't very big, after all. But anyway I was pretty relaxed, n'he and I got into some pretty serious talk, n'then he lowered his voice and told me that he wasn't who he looked to be."

"Was it somebody who died?" The image came to him of Abigail sitting in the car, looking scared.

"I guess that's how they work," she said.

"They can take somebody who just died, and fix them so they function again?"

"The thing is, it has to be somebody who is pretty isolated. Otherwise, there'd be all these relationships they'd have to deal with."

"Abigail didn't seem to have many relationships, except for that one guy." Walter sighed. "When he came there and found her dead, he was really shook up."

"I found my dad two years ago," she said quietly, "on the floor of his shop. I had nobody to call. My mom died years ago."

"No brothers or sisters?"

"No."

"Sorry for your loss," he said, at a loss for words.

"Thank you."

"What do you think they want?" Walter asked.

"Just to watch us, I think. They don't know anything about human emotions or relationships or stuff like that. They're just in their heads—so to speak."

They both laughed.

"My friend is really curious about sex," Jez said, smiling.

Walter lowered his voice. "You say they told you everything."

She nodded, that smile of conspiracy on her face.

He looked down. "It was like the woman had just discovered how to do it. She didn't hesitate, she just went for it, like she'd been doing it all along."

"Probably Abigail had."

He looked down. "I hadn't done it in six years."

"But you still knew how."

He laughed. Then he sighed. "Woke something up in me."

"This is a very weird conversation," Jez said.

"Isn't it."

"Will you talk to him?"

"Your friend?"

"Nothing to worry about," she said. "He's a pussy cat."

"Lemme think about it."

Walter waited another week before calling Jez. "I don't know what they expect from me," he said.

"Don't worry."

"This is very weird."

"You can do it. All they want is to talk with you—about yourself."

Walter blurted, "Am I going to die, and they want my body?"

Jez laughed, longer than Walter was comfortable with it. "Relax, friend. No, they don't want your body." Then she added an afterthought: "I don't think."

"Jez, I want to be straight with you," he said. "There's a part of me that's curious as hell. And another part that's scared shitless."

"Yep."

"I feel like I'm in way over my head."

"Yep."

He laughed. "You are something else, you know it?"

"Never was much of a standard model."
"It's like I can say anything to you."
"Might as well."
"What's that mean?" Holding his phone with a hunched-up shoulder, Walter was toying with a carpenter's pencil, creating a shaded drawing on a blueprint.
"You don't owe me anything. I ain't never going to be your lover."
"It's like you're a friend, and I don't even know you."
"You want to just forget this whole thing?"
"Too late."
"Okay, can you come to my place about five?"
Walter took a deep breath. "Okay."
She hung up without another word.

Later, he sat in his car, still in front of his house. *I'm gonna die,* he thought. *I'm in the middle of a thing like that movie with Scarlett Johansson, 'Under the Skin'. Jez is a real Jezebel, leading me to my death.*
But he laughed, thinking about how different Jez was from Scarlett Johansson. *Abigail might have gotten me with sex, but not this butch woman. Wonder if she's ever ...*
He started the car.

Walter pulled into the driveway and parked behind two pickup trucks. Jez's truck was old and rusted; the other one a late-model, clean and unblemished. He went to the back door—it seemed more appropriate in an old place like this.
Jez smiled at him when she opened the door. "Knew you'd come," she said. "We're in the parlor."
"Walter, meet Freddy." She gestured to Walter to sit in an overstuffed chair.

The Hitchhiker

Freddy looked young, maybe about thirty, short scruffy beard, hair just a little long. A journeyman, used to working with his hands. Jeans torn at the knees. His chambray shirt had never been ironed since it was new. "Hi, Walter," he said in a slight Tennessee accent. There was nothing about this man to reveal how different he actually was.

Walter didn't know what to say. He waited for Jez to break the ice.

"Walter is just a little bit anxious," she said finally.

"I need some help," said Freddy. "Jez thinks you might be able to help me."

"I'm about to freak out," Walter admitted, "but I'll hear what you have to say."

"I'm here to learn about people. We don't mean no harm to anybody."

Walter frowned. "First I need to know about you. I've already met one of your kind, and that went all right."

Freddy smiled. "One of us, you say."

"Well, didn't I?"

"I guess you could say that."

Jez spoke up, "I say 'they' a lot, but I think it's more complicated than that."

"I think I'm in over my head," said Walter.

"No you're not," said Jez, "no more'n me."

"Jez calls me 'him' a lot," said Freddy. "That's okay, if it makes it any easier for you. You know that 'male' and 'female' are strange concepts for us. Abigail told you that we all come from a single 'song'. Songs spring from us and grow into new individuals."

Walter frowned. "That's what she said."

"It's the closest word we know in English to how we multiply." Those words, coming out in that Tennessee accent, seemed very strange. "We appear to you in these

43

separate forms—these bodies—in order to communicate better with you."

Jez laughed. "That's how Freddy and I connected in the beginning—neither of us understands what sex is all about."

"I'm sure no expert," said Walter, resting a hand on his knee to stop its shaking. "In school I learned about how sexual activity is only one way life replicates itself on Earth. It seems to work pretty good." He chuckled. "Works for me, although I don't have any children."

Freddy smiled. "It was very interesting, when it happened between you and Abigail."

Walter felt his neck becoming warm. He cleared his throat. "Well, since you know all about that already," and he looked quickly at Jez, "Abigail was very—"

"Sexy?" asked Jez.

He nodded, blushing.

"Would a child grow from that action, if Abigail had not been allowed to die?" Freddy sat hunched forward, elbows on his knees, watching Walter carefully.

"You just let her die? Just like that?" Walter felt anger rising inside him. At the same time, he was aware of a strange mixture of emotions, thinking about Abigail.

"She had already died," Freddy said gently. "We let her go because her heart was very damaged. She would not have lived long. She was the wrong vehicle for us."

Walter took a deep breath and let it out. "Not every sexual act results in children." He was aware that he was trying to keep from talking about sex and Abigail.

"It seemed to be a very intense experience for both of you."

Walter scratched his head, trying to find words. "Yes, sometimes it is."

After a moment of silence, he looked up at Freddy and said, "You said 'we.' You've been saying 'we' but you

Walter shook his head and took a bite. "When he saw I was angry, he got a little hot himself."

"Shootout at the OK Corral," laughed Shep.

"I'm not laughin'," said Charlie. "We could be facing the end of the world or something."

Walter shrugged.

"We better get back to work," said Shep, "or we won't have jobs to go to—in case the world doesn't end."

As the three of them left the restaurant, Shep said, "You know how they always ask—if you know you're going to die in a short time, what would you want to be doing in the meantime."

"Ain't funny," muttered Charlie.

That afternoon Walter sat in his cubicle, thinking. *I don't think those guys really believe this. I'm not sure I believe it myself. If it's true, we could be in deep shit. But what the hell can we do? Freddy and his kind have all the cards. They know what they're doing, and we don't.*

By the time he got off work, he felt resigned to whatever was going to happen. But he had to know. He would get in touch with Jez again.

"Thought you might have skipped out," she said when he phoned her.

"No place to hide," he said.

Jez laughed. "If you spend more time with Freddy you might feel easier."

"I mean it—I can't hide. I can't walk away. I have to know what's going to happen."

"They pegged you right, didn't they?"

"What's that mean?" The conversation was making Walter nervous.

said—the way I heard it—you're not separate individuals."

Freddy grinned. "It's to make it easier for you. When I say 'I' it's mostly to refer to this body, that you know as Freddy."

"Then there's something else," Walter said. "When I was with Abigail, she said, 'I wish I were Abigail.' Was that you?"

Freddy ran his fingers through his hair. "The feeling was Abigail's." To Walter's look of bewilderment, he added, "Emotions and feelings are strange to us."

"Song—you used the word 'song' as though it meant something very special to you. Isn't that emotion?"

Jez laughed, and looked at Freddy. "See, didn't I tell you?"

Walter's mind kept jumping around among the three or four different feelings he was experiencing. Finally, he said what he really wanted to know: "Okay, here it is—what do you plan to do here? Are you going to take over the Earth and kill us all, or turn us into your herd of animals, or simply occupy our bodies and perform some kind of theater play?"

Freddy smiled again. "You seem to be tense."

"Goddamn right I'm tense! I don't know how all this is going to turn out."

"We're here just to observe you."

"What's your objective?"

"Interesting," Freddy said, in a tone like a college professor watching an experiment run. "Freddy is feeling something, an arousal."

"Christ!" Walter almost shouted. "That's what you said when you were in Abigail!"

Jez looked quickly at him. "I think Freddy is reacting to your anger."

Suddenly embarrassed, Walter slumped back in the chair. His memory of Abigail, her vulnerability, almost sweet innocence, played through his mind. He saw her touch her abdomen with a kind of curiosity. And then she had said softly, "I know what the feeling is now."

He shook his head. "It's too much. I can't deal with it." He stood up and looked at Jez. "Do you get it, Jez?"

She smiled. "It's something, isn't it?"

"Do you know what they are doing here?" He turned to Freddy. "How many of you are there?"

Freddy seemed perplexed. "You mean—"

"How many bodies are you inhabiting right now?"

"No human is being harmed. We're just here to observe."

"I don't believe you!" Walter turned and left the house. In his car, he took a deep breath and let it out before starting the engine. *What kinda shit am I into? I can't believe this! How come I'm the one they picked to question? They could be just leading us on, and in the end will end us all! If they are anything, they are not like us.*

W alter went to work the next week feeling as though the world was going to end very soon, but he didn't know what to do with the feelings. He tried hard to keep focused on his work, as though if he could ignore the situation, it wasn't really there.

But at lunch with Charlie and Shep, he had to say something: "You know that thing I talked about, that woman I found on the highway?"

Shep and Charlie stopped eating and stared at him. "You mean your alien visitor?" asked Shep, a grin on his face.

"You're still convinced, are you?" said Charlie.

"Had another experience," Walter said, and briefly described his meeting Jez and Freddy.

"Holy shit!" said Charlie.

"They're here," Walter said. "They could be all around us. You can't tell by looking at them." He sighed quickly. "And it may not even be 'them.' I couldn't get straight whether it's one huge being, with just parts occupying separate humans, or if it's a lot of them. The ones I talked to seemed to be the same, uh, person or whatever it is."

"You mean the same alien in the woman and in the man?"

"They're not used to the whole idea of different sexes. They kept asking me how that works." Walter still couldn't admit to his friends that he had had sex with Abigail.

Shep laughed. "Didn't you offer to demonstrate?"

Charlie was frowning. "I wouldn't be able to get it up for an alien—creeps me out just thinking about it."

"You say they could be all around us," said Shep. "What are they up to?"

"Don't have a clue. Freddy and Abigail both said they mean us no harm."

"Wonder if the government knows about them," Charlie said.

"Probably do," Shep answered, "but they wouldn't tell us because everybody'd panic."

"Maybe we *should* panic," said Walter, staring at hi uneaten sandwich. "I don't know what to do."

"You said the woman had died, and they just too over her body and brought her back to life," said Charl "How'd they get inside Freddy?"

"I didn't ask." Walter picked up his sandwich. " pissed me off."

"You got pissed?" Shep thought that was funny. " pull out your ray gun and threaten to zap him?"

The Hitchhiker

"You have integrity."
He was silent.
"Can you meet him tomorrow evening? At my place?"
"All right."

The next day Walter pulled into Jez's drive and parked behind the two pickup trucks. He let himself into her house without knocking, and found them in the parlor as before. He sat in the same overstuffed chair and waited.
"I'm glad you came," said Freddy.
Jez simply smiled at him.
"What do you want from me?" Walter asked, his voice subdued.
"Tell me about love," said Freddy.
"What?" Walter was startled. He had half-expected questions about sex, about male and female creating new humans by copulating. Physical mating. Biology.
Freddy leaned forward, his elbows on his knees. "You are one human, and I need your individual view. Others, we know, have different points of view. I need only yours. Tell me what love means to you."
Walter cleared his throat. "I'm not any expert."
"I know that." Freddy waited.
"I'm not a very good subject for that question. I was married until six years ago, when my wife left me."
"Did you love her?"
"Yes." Walter sighed. "I think I still do."
"But you hate her, too, don't you?" said Jez.
Walter looked over at the woman. He started to say something, then stopped.
"Is love related to hate?" asked Freddy.
"For me," Walter began, "love is feeling strongly pulled toward someone else, wanting to be near that person, willing to give up other things, other people." He

stopped, frowning. "That sounds so shallow! Love is deep."

Suddenly Walter felt something rise up in his throat. He thought of Daniele, and his old grief gripped him again as though all that were just yesterday.

"What—" Freddy began, but Walter stopped him with a gesture.

He took a deep breath. His voice grating, he said, "It's like the other person is a part of you. She completes you. And at the same time you are willing to give up everything else for her sake." He was thinking about Daniele, picturing her in her favorite chair, smiling at him, open to him—totally vulnerable to him.

"You are feeling something," Freddy said quietly. Freddy was suddenly the therapist, coaxing it out of him.

It was too intense for Walter. He cleared his throat. "Of course there are different kinds of love," he said. "Love for your children, love for your parents, for good friends, for mankind."

Freddy smiled. "You shifted. You're not talking about yourself."

"It's been six years," Walter sighed. "I thought I was over her—the dependency part."

Jez said, "Love is taking and giving."

"Yes."

"You said you still love her," said Freddy.

Walter smiled wryly. "That's the giving part. That's easy, once the hurt is healed. Forgiveness."

"The taking part is what hurts?"

Walter looked at him. "I thought you said you didn't know anything about love."

"We're learning."

"So am I," said Jez.

Walter turned to her. "And you said you didn't understand love."

"I said sex," she answered. I do know about love—a little."

"You know about loss?"

Her face was serious. "You betcha."

Walter was beginning to pick up something from Jez. The image he'd had, of this "butch woman" had been too simple. "Tell me."

"He was my god," she said.

He waited for more.

"He taught me everything I knew. When my mom died, he was all I had." She took a deep breath and let it out. "Then he died."

"I'm sorry."

"He loved me," she said, looking out the window, "he gave me all he could, but he couldn't know all the time what I needed."

"Maybe that's why Daniele left," Walter said. "I couldn't give her everything she needed."

Freddy looked at Walter. "How do you do it, you humans? How do you know what others have in their minds?"

Jez chuckled. "Not a problem for you, is it?"

Freddy looked at her questioningly.

"You are not separate like we are," she said.

Walter turned to Freddy, "We have to do it just like we're doing it here, right now. We talk. We touch. We use body language."

"Body language?"

"It's how you hold yourself with someone else," Jez explained, "how you gesture, your facial expressions."

"The last time we were together," Freddy said to Walter, "I felt something from you. I couldn't describe it in words, but then you expressed anger—pretty clearly."

Jez laughed. "That he did."

"That feeling I had then. How did that happen?"

Walter scratched his head. "I've read that we are very good at reading each other. I guess that's what you felt. You were picking up subtle vibes—I don't know what to call it, exactly. Vibes—vibrations—is what some people call it.

"And all that happens whenever people are together?"

"Some people close themselves off so you can't read them, and some people aren't good at reading." Walter watched Freddy, wondering how much of this he understood.

"When you were with Abigail," Freddy said, holding Walter's gaze, "it was more than simple physical connecting, wasn't it?"

Walter blushed. "You dig deep, don't you?"

Jez laughed.

Freddy furrowed his brow. "You were vibrating?"

That made both Walter and Jez laugh out loud.

"I was, indeed. Good sex always includes good vibes." He took a breath and looked at Jez. "I can't believe I'm talking like this to a stranger."

"You're not closed," said Freddy.

"When you were in Abigail," Walter began, then paused. "You *were* in Abigail, weren't you?"

Freddy smiled.

Walter looked across the room, anywhere except at Freddy. "It's hard to get my mind around all that."

"Wow," said Jez softly.

"When you were in Abigail, you said, 'I wish I were Abigail.' And yet you say you don't know about emotions. I wanted to ask you the other day about that. You said humans have emotions, as though you don't."

Freddy looked at him without speaking.

"Wasn't that emotion?"

"I don't know. Something."

Walter opened his hands, as though to open the idea. "It's like people—people I know, anyway—communicate on different levels at the same time. The top level, the superficial level, is the words they use and the deliberate body language. The words you can look up in the dictionary to find out what they mean."

He paused. "Under that level can be a number of levels of meaning. Deeper meaning. Like irony, for example. Irony is a meaning that can be the opposite of the top level of meaning. I can say to you, 'You are an honorable man' but mean that I think you are not honorable. It's only effective if the person being addressed understands the deeper meaning. If you have just cheated someone, and I say that you are honorable, both of us know it isn't true." Walter looked at Freddy. "Does that make sense to you?"

Freddy was silent for a moment. "No," he said finally.

"Beneath that layer of meaning could be other layers. I might say those words to you and be quoting someone else, who said them to someone else, with reference to some other situation. If we both know about that other situation and that statement that I've quoted, it might mean something even deeper."

"I'm trying to understand."

"It takes years to learn these things," Walter said. "You can't be expected to learn them easily. You need a lot of experiences to integrate such knowledge."

"I'm trying to understand, too," Jez said. "You're over my head."

Walter smiled. "Jez just said I was over her head. That's another figure of speech, which means something different from the dictionary meaning of the words. It means that what I just described is beyond her understanding."

"You're over my head," said Freddy.

53

They all laughed.

"I don't know what else to say," said Walter. "When you first revealed yourself to me, you said you were here—or there, in Abigail—to observe. I don't know what else to tell you."

Jez, looking at Freddy, said, "In the beginning, I thought you were super-intelligent, you knew everything, but I'm beginning to think you're short a thing or two."

Freddy laughed. "I get your figure of speech. You mean we need to learn a lot more than 'a thing or two'."

"Bingo," said Jez.

Walter stood up. "There are a lot of people who are a lot wiser than I am. You need to contact them."

Freddy was silent.

"Freddy," said Jez, "tell me something?"

"You mean, you're asking me to tell you something—right?"

She grinned at him. "How did you get into Freddy?"

"He was electrocuted. He touched an electric wire while working at his trade."

"And in that instant, you took over." She pursed her lips, thinking.

"Yes."

"He must have been an all right guy."

"I don't know." Freddy looked thoughtful.

"What will happen to his body?"

"He will be found. Someone will take him away."

"Feels weird," she said.

"That's how it's done," said Walter. "You said we will not be harmed."

"Yes."

"Then I am going back to my life." he said, starting for the door.

Jez followed him. "You haven't showed me your shop," she said quietly.

He turned to her. "You're in my life—if you want to be."

She put a hand on his arm. "I do want to be."

"Good." Then he raised his voice. "Good bye, Freddy."

"Thank you, Walter," he said in that strange Tennessee accent.

Walter went to his truck and backed out of the drive.

Three

Michael looked up from the desk. She was pretty and slim, even though, to him, a little "older."

She held out a coupon. "I'm Abby DeVoe," she said. "I understand this gives me a discount on five visits to your gym."

"Indeed it does," he said, pulling a paper from a drawer. "Would you fill out this application form?"

After the paperwork was finished, Michael showed Abby around the workout room, demonstrating each machine. On those that required adjustments, he had her try out the machine herself, and wrote down the appropriate numbers for her.

"I'm not on the staff here," he told her. "I'm just filling in for the secretary while she's at lunch. But I'm pretty much a regular here. I come a lot of evenings after work, and usually on Saturdays. I like how my body feels after a workout."

"I know I should take better care of my body," she said. "That's why I'm here."

"Well, anytime I can help you, just let me know."

After seeing each other at the gym occasionally, they began to chat more, and sometimes went out for coffee together before heading home. In time, friendship developed.

He'd never met a woman like Abby. Vivacious and impulsive, she acted much younger than she looked, but she was also thoughtful, unlike most of the women his own age, whom he thought to be often frivolous and empty. Their conversations were about important things, like climate change and the Middle East, and how individuals could cope with the fast pace of the world.

The Hitchhiker

She was an editor in a small magazine publishing company. "All day I read about farm equipment, but my heart is in poetry."
"You write poetry?"
She laughed. "A little, but nothing I want to show to anybody."
"I have to admit that I don't understand most poetry I've read. I like to read short fiction—stories that don't get too mysterious."
After several months, the two became intimate, usually going to her apartment after dinner together. Occasionally, he slept over.
"You said you like gin," she said one evening, going to the pantry. "I bought some tonic water, too."
"Terrific." He stood in the doorway, watching her.
"I don't like to drink alone." She took down two glasses and filled them with ice from the refrigerator. Turning to look at him, she said, "Sometimes I get depressed, and that's a bad time to drink alcohol."
"Yes," he said. "Why do you get depressed?"
She smiled. "I don't know. I don't often have company here, in spite of the fact that I get lonely sitting in there watching television."
As she poured gin into the glasses, he said, "If you keep the gin in the freezer, you can enjoy just a quick shot once in a while to pick you up." He laughed. "Especially that Bombay Sapphire."
She smiled. "Is this good gin?"
"Very good."
She handed him a drink and they touched glasses. "Thank you," he said.

In the next few weeks, their evenings in her apartment became more and more sexual. Abby was quite enthusiastic as a lover, and Michael was delighted.

Michael emptied the glass of wine he'd been nursing, and looked around the room. The other diners were laughing and chatting together, most having finished their meals and were preparing to leave.

Abby had never been this late. They alternated their dinner locations between Braille, where she lived, and the city, his home territory, since there were few restaurants in between them that they liked. Ever since they had become close, they talked about one of them moving nearer, but their jobs were important to both of them.

He looked at his watch. She'd suggested this restaurant for tonight because of the atmosphere. But she was an hour late. He phoned her apartment. There was no answer. *On her way,* he guessed. He promised himself that he would try to persuade her to buy a cell phone, something that she had insisted was "too technical" for her.

Michael ordered another glass of Chardonnay and waited. He'd already looked at the menu and chosen what he would eat, but didn't order anything, nibbling on the bread the waiter had brought.

After the second glass of wine, he tried her phone again. This time a man answered.

Startled, Michael hesitated. "May I speak with Abigail?"

The man sounded older. "She can't come to the phone right now. Do you know Abigail?"

Michael hesitated. "Yes. She and I were supposed to meet this evening."

"What's your name?"

"Michael. Abigail and I were supposed to meet at eight o'clock, and she hasn't shown up yet. Is she there? Is she all right?"

The man's tone worried Michael, "I think it might be good if you came here."

Michael felt foreboding rising up inside. "What's wrong? Who are you?"

"Please come." And the phone clicked off.

His heart pounding, he signaled the waiter for the check, paid and immediately left the restaurant.

On the drive to Braille, he tried to remember if Abby had other men friends. Who would that be at her apartment? The guy hadn't said she was or was not there, only that she couldn't come to the phone. A policeman or emergency worker would surely have identified himself.

By the time Michael knocked on her door, he was shaking with apprehension.

A strange man opened the door and, apparently knowing who Michael was, pointed to the bedroom. "She's in there," he said simply. "She died in her sleep."

Michael rushed into the bedroom, where Abby lay on top of the covers, appearing as though she were asleep. He felt her neck for a pulse. All his fear boiled up into sobbing grief, and he threw himself on her body. He wasn't even aware that the man slipped out without saying anything. Later, Michael found a note that told where to find Abby's car on the highway from the city. Her keys were with the note.

How did she die? Who was that man? Why didn't he stay and explain anything? What should I do? Michael sat down in Abby's living room to collect himself.

Finally, he decided that he had to report this to the police. He dialed 9-1-1.

While the emergency crew collected Abby's body and wheeled it down to the EMS vehicle, two plainclothes policemen questioned Michael. He told them everything he knew, and showed them the note.

"Do you know where this is?" asked one, pointing to the note.

"Yes, approximately," Michael answered.

"We'll run out there and see. Are those her keys to the car?"

"Yes, I think so."

"These other two keys—do you know what they are to?"

Michael pulled his own keys out of his pocket and compared one to Abigail's keys. "This one is her apartment." He gestured toward the door. "The other one, I don't know. Maybe it's to her storage locker in the basement."

"I don't see any evidence of foul play," said one detective. "But we need you to be available for more questions, okay?"

"Sure." He gave them his business card from work.

"Okay, you can go. When we find out anything, we'll let you know."

Driving back home, Michael felt only sadness. Abby had become such a close friend—and lover.

Approaching the city, he saw flashing lights ahead, and recognized Abby's car already being loaded onto a carrier. He didn't stop.

The next day, he phoned the Braille police and asked about the investigation. They told him that Abby had in all likelihood suffered a heart attack. The emergency room in the city had told them that she had been brought in by a man who then left with her, apparently to take her to her home. Everything fit together, and it was being treated as a "natural causes" case. They wanted to talk with the man who had brought her to the E.R. They said they had his name and address.

The Hitchhiker

For days, Michael couldn't stop thinking about Abby. They hadn't gotten to the stage in their relationship where they talked about the future, but he had often thought of her with feelings that approached love. He hadn't been in a romantic relationship for some time, and she offered him both comfort and excitement.

She hadn't revealed much about her past, and the single photograph on her piano showed an elderly couple who she said were her parents. With his phone, Michael had taken a selfie of the two of them, and had it printed and framed for her. The next time he had visited, the picture was on the piano next to her parents.

The gym seemed haunted. Every time a woman came in, he looked, half expecting it to be Abby.

He called the Braille police, asking about her, and about the strange man who had been in her apartment that night. On the phone, they seemed reluctant to tell him much, so one day he took off work and drove there to talk to someone in person.

"He was the one who had taken her into the E.R.," they told him. "We interviewed him, and he seemed straightforward, a good Samaritan who saw her on the highway and stopped to help. He said he didn't want to get involved—that's why he left when you arrived."

They also said that they had tracked down her mother, who was in a nursing home in Battle Creek. Her Alzheimer's prevented her from giving much information. The officer smiled. "Your mystery woman is still pretty much a mystery," she said.

"Can you give me the number of the man?" Michael asked. "At least I'd like to thank him for taking care of her."

"Can't do that," she said, but opened the file on her desk and half-turned it. "Excuse me," she said, "I have to get something from the back office."

When she left the room, Michael looked at the open file and wrote on a scrap of paper "Walter Anderson" and the phone number. When the officer returned, he thanked her and left.

An answering machine met his call. He left his name and number without explaining why he'd called.

A week later, Michael answered his own phone to hear, "This is Walter Anderson. You called me last week."

"Yes," Michael said, "I've been wanting to talk with you about Abigail DeVoe."

"I don't know her," Walter said, and hung up.

Michael called his number again. After four rings, Walter answered.

"I don't mean to cause you any trouble," Michael said. "I talked with the Braille police, and they said they had talked with you but didn't think there was any problem."

"They did talk with me, and I told them everything I knew," Walter said. "I just found her sitting in her car and I took her to her home."

"They also said you took her to the emergency room. I'm grateful for that."

"What's your connection with Abigail?"

"Just good friends," Michael said.

There was a long pause in the conversation. Then Michael asked, "You were with her when she died?"

"Yes."

"Uh—was she in any pain?"

"Not that I could tell. It was quite sudden. The doctors said she had a heart condition."

"Why didn't you stay long enough to just tell me what had happened?"

"I was a stranger. I didn't want to get involved."

Michael was silent for a moment. Then he said, "She wanted to write poetry."

It was Walter's turn to be silent. "Do you want to meet for coffee?"

"I'd like that," Michael said.

"There's a Denny's downtown on High Street. Do you know where that is?"

Walter recognized the young man immediately. He signaled to him.

After they had seated themselves in a booth, Walter said, "I guess you're curious about me. I'm curious about Abigail."

He explained that he had taken her home, but when he went into the bathroom, she apparently lay down on the bed and just died there. When he emerged from the bathroom, she showed no sign of life.

Michael sagged visibly.

"The E.R. recommended that she see her regular doctor as soon as possible," Walter said. "I guess it was more serious than they thought."

The two men sat silently for a time.

Then Walter said, "When you called, she seemed to be kind of out of it, like she wasn't functioning very well. I thought she should have someone there who knew her, at least. I didn't know what to do for her."

"Yeah," said Michael. "When you left, I was really confused. I didn't know her parents or anything. I thought the best thing was to report it to the police."

"She seemed like a nice woman." Walter thought about that night, as he had slowly realized that Abigail was not really Abigail, and he had felt completely lost. "I was glad you called—at least you knew who she was."

"I've never had to deal with a situation like that," Michael said. "I've never even seen a dead person except my grandmother, when I was a kid."

Walter wanted to tell this young man about Abigail, the Abigail he had encountered the night she had died, but there seemed no way it could make any sense. Even now, he had a hard time trying to understand what had happened.

"She seemed confused," he said, "the whole evening. I guess she had a stroke, and it took away some of her mental capacity."

"Her mind was always so sharp," Michael said.

"Have you tried to find out if she had any family?"

"No." He screwed up his face. "I thought we were really close, but she never mentioned her family. There was just one photo in her apartment—but I guess you saw that—of her parents, I guess."

"Probably the police would try to locate them. They'd go through her things to find out."

"Thanks for talking with me, at least. You were kind of a mystery man."

Walter pushed his coffee spoon around on the table. "The police called me, but I couldn't tell them anything except what I've told you. They didn't seem concerned about me."

Michael put his elbows on the table, his hands clasping his coffee cup. "I don't mean to raise any questions or put you on the spot, but—"

Walter looked up, surprised.

"There were a couple of glasses on the coffee table, and some frozen food containers in the kitchen." He gave

The Hitchhiker

a little nervous laugh. "I gather that you two had something to eat and drink. You didn't mention that."

Walter looked at him for a moment, then said, "I was trying to get through to her. I thought she might be hungry. We both ate."

"I'm surprised that she ate that. She was a vegetarian."

Walter took a deep breath. "She didn't say anything." He was getting uncomfortable.

"She had both meat and veggie dishes in the freezer, 'cause I eat meat. But she never did, that I know of." Michael was looking intently at Walter.

Walter shrugged. "She didn't seem to know how to eat." Then he stopped, regretting what he'd just said. "I mean, maybe she was confused."

"I keep thinking that there's something you aren't telling me." Michael leaned on one elbow.

Walter was now very uncomfortable. "Uh, I can't think of anything more. We went to her apartment and I was trying to find out if I could call anybody for her. Then you called, and I thought you could handle it."

"And you both had gin and tonics," Michael said. "The gin bottle was out on the table, and she always keeps it in the freezer. The glasses still had ice in them."

Walter remembered that evening, when he had to show Abigail how to drink. She seemed so innocent then, almost as though she were in a dream. Then he remembered, for the hundredth time, how she had jumped on him and begun loosening his belt. His face felt hot.

"I don't mean to put you on the spot," said Michael, "but maybe I do. Was she drunk? Did you get her drunk?" He sat back in his seat. "Did you tell me to come there because she had passed out drunk?"

"No!" Walter felt anger rising, and the hair on the back of his neck stood up. "Wouldn't the autopsy show that?"

"They didn't let me see the autopsy report," said Michael.

"Well, they sure didn't ask me such a question."

Michael looked down. "I'm sorry," he said. "I just feel like there's something more to this. I guess I'm just paranoid. I'm sorry."

Walter took a breath. "Yeah, I fixed us both a gin and tonic. It wasn't even very strong. Couldn't have had anything to do with her death. I don't think."

Michael's eyes were misting up. "I'm sorry," he said softly. "I miss her—a lot."

Walter relaxed a little. "I understand. I only knew her for an hour or so. She seemed a nice person, but she was obviously very ill."

"She never told me anything about a heart condition. She worked out on the machines at the gym, and seemed to handle that pretty well."

Walter sighed. Then he looked directly at Michael. "I may regret this," he said quietly. And then he told the other man what had happened that night—everything except the sex.

Michael, at first, returned Walter's gaze with widening eyes. Then gradually his face betrayed a growing anger. "I don't know what you think you're doing," he said. "I don't believe any of that shit!"

Walter sighed again. "Yeah. It was a mistake. Forget the whole thing."

Both men got up from the booth and left the restaurant without exchanging another word. Walter stopped at the cashier stand and paid for the coffee. By the time he reached his car, Michael had gone.

The Hitchhiker

The coroner of Braille County eventually issued a report on the death of Abigail DeVoe, calling it a heart attack.

The police notified the manager of the condo where she had lived that her unit could be cleaned out for another resident. The manager hired a local auction company to come in and remove everything. It was taken temporarily to a garage-type storage unit.

A month later, Walter got a flyer in the mail announcing an auction at a storage facility. The flyer had been mailed in a plain business envelope with no return address. In the list of lockers to be auctioned off, one unit had been circled with a felt-tip pen. Walter almost threw it away before noticing that the zip code on the envelope was that of Braille.

Curious, he looked up the location of the storage facility. It was just outside the town of Braille.

For two days, he left the flyer on his desk at home. Then he picked it up, intending to throw it into the trash until he noticed that the auction was to be that day. Instead of discarding it, he pocketed the flyer and drove to Braille.

The contents of six units in the little facility were to be auctioned off. No one was allowed to enter past the yellow tape across each open door.

A small crowd of people had gathered for the auctions, drifting back and forth along the line of units and peering into the interiors, some with flashlights.

Walter identified the unit that had been circled on his flyer, and looked inside at a collection of boxes and furniture. Nothing caught his attention. It was simply a bunch of unremarkable junk, somebody's belongings that had not been worth paying for the monthly charges. Only two or three people took any interest in the unit.

He waited until the auctioneer got to that unit to begin the sale. "What can you tell me about this one?" he asked.

The auctioneer seemed uninterested. "All I can tell you is somebody died, and nobody claimed their stuff."

Walter got up as close as the tape would allow and peered into the unit again. In the back, behind a stack of boxes, stood a small piano. Someone else was standing alongside him, and noticed the piano at the same time. "There's a boat anchor for you," he said. "Can't give those things away these days." The man walked away, but Walter continued to stare at the piano. *That was in Abigail's apartment,* he thought. *These were her belongings!*

The mysterious flyer, with the storage unit number circled, suddenly became meaningful. Someone had sent it to him because these things belonged to Abigail. His heart pounded. He didn't dwell on the question of who had sent the flyer—the important thing was that he needed to see what her apartment had held.

When the auctioneer began the litany, Walter made the first bid. Only two other people bid, and when he had raised the bid to a hundred dollars, both of them dropped out.

"You got four days to get this stuff out of here," the auctioneer told him as an assistant took Walter's money, name and address. "Every bit of it has to be out of here by, uh, next Wednesday. Otherwise, we will remove it and bill you for the transportation to the landfill."

Although he wanted to explore the contents of the storage unit he had just purchased, Walter didn't want to do it so publicly. He obtained a padlock from the storage

The Hitchhiker

facility manager, and after securing the unit he went back home.

The next morning, he returned to the storage unit. Carefully sorting through the boxes, he separated Abigail's clothing and kitchen ware, all of which he would give to Goodwill Industries. What he was most interested in were the boxes of personal papers and books. These he put into two small boxes and carried them to his truck, along with a small end table that looked good enough to refinish.

On his way back home, he stopped at a small church near the storage facility. Several people stood around outside, evidently socializing after the Sunday service.

"Would you be interested in obtaining as a gift a small spinet-style piano?" he asked.

The men talked among themselves, and finally said that they might want it, if it was in good condition.

Walter drove two of the men back to the storage unit, where they agreed to take the piano off his hands if they could load it into his truck right then.

Satisfied, Walter drove back home with his boxes, wondering what they would tell him.

At home, with papers scattered around the living room, he began to construct a picture of the woman to whom he had become somehow attached.

Abigail lived what appeared to be an austere life. Her equity in the condo was miniscule. No doubt the owner of the property would foreclose after a suitable time and resell it to someone else. She had a checking account containing less than a hundred dollars. A file folder contained a few receipts from retail stores.

Walter found an address book, but many of the entries had been crossed out, a few of which had other addresses penciled in. None appeared to be local except the nursing home where her mother lived.

A few letters from other people, dated years before, had been collected in a file folder. Nothing in them suggested close relationships.

Another file folder contained her condo contract, dated two years before, the title to her car and a legal document stapled together that certified that she had been divorced from a man named Henry DeVoe a dozen years before. The decree originated in Dallas, Texas.

A paper file portfolio contained typewritten documents, some of which were poems and others short stories, mostly unfinished. Penciled changes had been made on most of the documents.

Walter felt vaguely disappointed. He didn't know what he had expected, but Abigail DeVoe seemed to have been a lonely sort of woman, with few friends and, evidently, a mother with dementia her only living relative.

After dinner, he put on some music and settled down with the file folder of her writings. The one piece that caught his attention was a story or memoir:

```
              Ian
         By Abigail Devoe

   Ian was a strange man. He was tall and
handsome, clean shaven but with long
sideburns, which reminded me of pictures
from the nineteenth century. We met as I was
bicycling through Mt. Airy Park in the fall.
The trees were turning, and the air was
cool.
   Ian was sitting on a park bench alongside
the trail. I stopped and we exchanged
pleasantries. "Just resting", he said. He
```

The Hitchhiker

told me he had been walking, but had just recovered from an injury resulting from an automobile accident, and he got tired easily. So we got into a long conversation.

At first I was uneasy with him because he spoke so strangely, as though he was speaking in a language foreign to him. Yet he didn't seem to have an accent, as most foreigners do. But after a while I felt more comfortable because he seemed friendly without prying.

I wondered if he had had brain injury in his accident, which could have caused his difficulties in speaking. You know how sometimes you forget a word that is familiar to you? Ian had a lot of those words, except if I tried to help him by suggesting words, he acted as though he'd never known the words. Like somebody from a foreign country.

He was intrigued with my bicycle, wondering how it managed to stay upright as I rode. I laughed, because bicycles are so common—every child has one, at some point in his or her life.

As we talked, he tried to tell me how his people multiplied—through some kind of "song". It was as though they didn't have males and females.

I couldn't imagine where these people might have lived. I've never heard of any race that didn't multiply from sexual intercourse.

After a while, I got a little nervous around him. He was just too different, even though he looked like an ordinary person. I got on my bike and resumed my ride. I never saw him again.

Donald Skiff

```
Ever since then, I've wondered
```

The writing stopped there, at the bottom of a page. Walter thought that there must be more pages, but they were not in the folder.
He went back and read the story again, feeling very strange. The way she described the man, it could have applied to her, that evening, as well. *Was Ian one of them? He must have been. When was that?* He couldn't shake the feeling, almost of *déjà vu*.
Most of the poems seemed to be just sketches, unfinished attempts of a beginning poet. One, however, revealed something else:

```
He thrusts inside me,
A wild animal
Who turns me into his kind.

We soar into the heaven
Together
Tasting ecstasy

And then deflated
Like children's balloons
To sleep in peace.
```

It reminded Walter again of that night. Something about Abigail had awakened him in ways he'd long forgotten.
Walter sighed, and closed the folder. *She knew,* he thought. *Or they knew her. She wrote that she never saw Ian again—but what about the poem?*
No, he decided, the poem could have been anybody. There were no dates on any of the pages.
Still. *What does it mean?*

The next day Walter took a sick day from work and drove his truck down to Braille, where he emptied out the storage unit, taking almost everything to a local Goodwill store. There was nothing else in the unit that interested him, even the photograph that had stood on her piano.

Jez's voice on the phone was somehow reassuring. "Hi, Friend," her message said. "I'm returning your call, and I'll be around the rest of today. Tomorrow I'm working at a construction site on the other side of town. You can get me in the evenings, though."

Walter, who had just gotten home from work, waited until after dinner before calling Jez back. "I've never showed you my shop," he told her. "When would you have time to come over and maybe share a dram or two?"

"I'll be pretty whacked out this week," she said, "with this site installation I'm doing. Can we make it next Sunday?"

"Perfect for me," he said. "Come for lunch. You still have my address?"

"Sure do. See you then."

That week Walter thought a lot about what he would say to Jez, and what she might say as well. He felt a kinship with her, and a trust that even though she was evidently in touch with *them*, she would respect his desire to avoid more contact with Freddy and his kind.

His discovery of Abigail's writing changed everything. How much of that was coincidence? That she might have had contact with one of them, and then when she died from a heart attack in her car, had they been observing her?

And who sent him that flyer about the storage facility auction? Was *he* being watched, even now?

On Friday after work, he debated whether to reveal any of this to Charlie and Shep. Jez had asked him not to say anything to others, although she didn't say why. But this was now a bigger thing than just Jez and Freddy.

"Why didn't you tell us you needed some help moving shit on Monday, Man?" Shep asked.

"Oh, I didn't know it was going to be so much. And a couple of guys from a church helped me with the piano."

"So what was all this stuff you had to move?" asked Charlie, tossing off his first shot of Patrón.

"Just some stuff in a storage locker that a friend couldn't pay any more to keep," Walter said.

"Where was this?"

Walter hesitated. "Braille."

"Braille," said Shep. "Isn't that where you were with that woman who died?"

"Was it her stuff?" asked Charlie.

Walter smiled. "Yeah."

"Didn't she have any relatives or anything to take care of it? Why you?"

Walter sighed. "I bought the contents of the storage unit," he admitted.

"You bought it?" Shep grinned. "Something you're not telling us about this babe? C'mon, Walter."

"I was just curious," said Walter.

"So did you turn up a hundred K stuffed in a mattress?"

"No, she didn't have anything of value," he lied.

"Man," said Charlie, "You've become something else since that shit went down. You're rattling on about aliens …"

"And now you got a thing about a dead woman," added Shep.

The Hitchhiker

The three were silent for a while, drinking tequila.
"You got any new ideas about these aliens?" asked Charlie.
"No."
"So they're not fixin' to take us down in the near future."
"I don't think so."
"Well," said Shep, "You'll let us know if we need to make our Last Will and Testament, right?"
Shep and Charlie exchanged glances.
Walter decided that there was nothing more to be said on the subject. Abigail's poem came up into his awareness for a moment—*these two guys would enjoy that poem*, he thought, *and understand nothing*.

Sunday morning Walter was nervous. He downed a straight shot of vodka to calm him down. He intended to show Abigail's writing to Jez, just so they could discuss the issues it brought up.
When she arrived, however, he first took her down to his basement shop. "You're a lot better equipped than I am," he said.
Jez looked over his machinery and his works in progress, and complimented him on his workmanship. She noticed the little end table he'd salvaged from Abigail's storage unit. "You didn't make that, though, did you?"
"No. I just thought I could refinish it."
"It's not up to your standards."
He laughed. "Thank you."
For lunch he made a mushroom omelet. As they ate, they chatted about woodworking.
Then he said, "I assume you're still in touch with Freddy."
She nodded without saying anything.

"I know I told you I didn't want to be involved with them anymore."

"Something's come up."

"Uh, yeah," he began, "you didn't send me a flyer from a storage facility, did you?"

She looked up quickly. "No."

"Somebody wanted me to know about the contents of Abigail's apartment."

She shook her head slowly, watching him.

"I was just curious about what she might have left," he said.

"And..."

"She must have been a pretty lonely person. There were almost no personal effects. But I bought the whole storage unit, and gave it away to a church and to Goodwill."

"Nothing you want to talk about?"

He went to his office and returned with the file folder. Without saying anything, he set it in front of her, and began clearing the table as she leafed through the pages.

"Lordy," she said, reading the memoir. Then she leafed through the poetry, pausing only momentarily at the erotic one.

Walter sat down across from her. "She knew about them," he said.

"Looks like it."

"Was she a marked woman?"

Jez looked up at him. "Do I think they did anything to her? No."

"But they knew her."

She shrugged. "I don't know what that would mean."

"Can't tell when these things were written," he said, gesturing toward the folder, "but maybe they had her under observation or something. Maybe the business when she had her heart attack in the car..." He stopped.

The Hitchhiker

She shrugged again. "Man, you've got an active imagination."

"Aren't you curious?"

Jez grinned. "Not like you."

"I think they sent me that flyer so I would go to the storage locker."

She sat back in the chair and looked at him.

"Only people I've told about her is the Braille police, and they wouldn't be sending me a flyer."

"What about your friend Michael?"

"Oh, shit!" Walter slumped in his chair. "How do they know about him?"

She grinned again. "I guess they do have you in their field of vision."

"That doesn't bother you?"

Another shrug. "Okay, Freddy did tell me about Michael. They've been interested in him because of Abigail."

"So you know I've talked with him." A bead of sweat rolled down his temple.

"Yeah."

"He didn't believe me."

"Yeah."

Walter's brow furrowed. "Were they listening in to our conversation?"

She didn't reply.

"Jesus Christ! Now I am worried!"

Jez sat upright and looked directly at him. "They aren't here to harm anybody."

"How do you know?"

That shrug. "Just do."

They sat in silence for a long while. Then Jez picked up the file folder and waved it. "What did you want me to see this for?"

Walter sighed.

"I didn't know about this," she said, "but I'm not surprised."

He frowned. "This isn't just one or two, uh, *incidents*. How many—*how big is this thing?*"

"I don't know," she said. "Is it any bigger a question than whether there's a heaven and hell?"

"Or whether there's a god?" He cupped his hands together into a big fist, pressed against his mouth.

"Pretty real, ain't it?" She had that conspiratorial smile on her face.

Walter sighed again, resigned. "At least God would know all about love, wouldn't he?"

They sat looking at each other.

Walter finally stood up. "You want coffee?"

Walter and Jez began occasional visits to each other's woodworking shops, chatting informally about their craft but seldom mentioning the alien being or beings that seemed to be observing the humans on Earth.

As with most budding friendships, their conversations gradually became more personal. He talked about his marriage and how he had pretty much shut down emotionally after his wife had left him.

Jez talked about her father, who had mentored her in woodworking and supported her emotionally through a difficult adolescence. After her mother had died, Jez had taken over the household duties for him, and they had spent most of their evenings watching television and talking shop.

"I ain't pretty," she admitted to Walter one evening over drinks. "I didn't think I had any chance to get a husband." She laughed. "Just never gave it much thought."

"Never dated?" Walter was careful to avoid talking about sex with her. She was different from other women he had known, and he wondered if she might be a lesbian.

She chuckled and shrugged. "I asked a fellow out once, when I was in high school, but that didn't go too well, and I never tried it again."

"No friendships?"

Jez closed one eye and looked at him. "I was pretty much a loner. Didn't fit in, didn't really try."

She paused. "Guess Freddy is the only friend I've had in a long time."

That startled Walter. "You call Freddy a friend?"

She frowned. "Yeah," she said. "What else?"

Walter looked away and took a deep breath. "Even if ..."

"You mean because he ain't, ah, *human?*"

Walter laughed. She was so genuine at that point, so *uncluttered,* that he couldn't help but like her. "I'm sorry," he said, "you're right. Even if Freddy isn't like us, you two have some kind of connection. I guess that's friendship—you accept each other as you are."

"Why not?" She seemed perplexed.

"You're right. When I was a kid, I had a dog, and he and I were best friends. We trusted each other more than anybody else in the world. He wasn't just a dog to me. I didn't have any brothers or sisters. Sam was *family.*"

Jez nodded. "Yeah, I get that. Freddy and me are like family, I guess. I don't push on him, and he don't push on me."

"What do you talk about?"

"Sometimes we don't even talk. I might fill him in on stuff he don't understand. He don't know a lot of stuff."

"Like what?"

"Like, stuff about why people act the way they do." She was silent for a moment. "I worry about him sometimes."

"Why is that?"

"He ain't well. I can tell. He sometimes has to stop and catch his breath. Funny, for a guy as young as he is, it's like he's an old man. Sometimes."

"He got folks?" Walter was also beginning to wonder about Freddy. Supposedly he'd been killed by electricity, and then brought back to life. *Like Abigail,* he thought

"Not as far as I know. He never said."

Their conversation trailed off into shop talk, and soon Jez left.

Four

They didn't talk for a couple of weeks, until one evening Jez phoned Walter. "Freddy's gone," she said, her voice catching on the last word.

"He left?"

"No, he just never showed up. We was supposed to install some cabinets over on Wooster Boulevard, but he never showed up."

"You try to call him?"

"No answer."

Walter's mind was running wild. *They've left him and gone to somebody else.* "You want to talk?"

She laughed half-heartedly. "You got any of that good tequila?"

"You betcha. Come on over."

Walter hadn't thought about the aliens in a while. The world hadn't changed. Nothing was reported in the newspapers, and nobody had said anything to remind him. When he did think about *them*, it was from a distance. He lived his life as he had before he found Abigail, worked in his shop and spent a little time with Shep and Charlie, mostly at the bar. They didn't talk about his adventures with the alien, or aliens—he still wasn't sure how to think about the visitors.

Jez was obviously upset when she arrived. Over tequila, she finally said, "I thought he would eventually go someplace else. Maybe he died, after all, and they didn't bring him back. But I thought we'd have a chance to say good bye." Her eyes glistened.

"You've had a lot of loss in your life, and you've had to deal with it alone," Walter said quietly.

"Yeah."

"Do you think they're still around?" He refilled their glasses while he waited for her to answer.

"Don't have a clue."

"You know," he began, "I've wondered if they were getting what they wanted from us. Freddy—or whatever he was—didn't seem to understand us. Oh, he could talk and carry on a conversation, but it was all pretty superficial."

She wiped her cheek with the back of her hand. "I don't understand *you*, sometimes," she said. You're way deeper than I am. All your talk about mirrors and levels of mind or whatever..."

"Sorry. I don't mean to go off on all that. Just how I'm thinking. I get curious. Like I'm curious about *them*. I stopped being scared, I guess. It seemed that Freddy wasn't going to do anything to us. I just wonder what they are, or were after."

She sipped from her glass. "Freddy and I could talk pretty good," she said. "He seemed—I don't know—*real*, somehow. Didn't put on airs. Just said what he thought."

Walter grinned. "Is that what I do? Put on airs?"

She waved a hand. "No, I didn't mean that. Sometimes you're over my head, but I think you're a real person."

"I have feelings," he said. "I don't always show them, but I try to be honest." Walter was aware of feeling the liquor.

She smiled. "They had you pegged right. Maybe they didn't get what they wanted from you, but I did."

"If he comes back—if *they* come back—I'd like to know."

"Okay." She stood up. "I got to move around a little bit. My back gets stiff just sitting."

Walter took a deep breath. "You know," he said, "when I first met you—well, you seem different to me now

The Hitchhiker

than you did at first. We could talk about wood working, but I thought that's all."

She smiled at him without speaking.

"There's a lot more to you than I thought. You were able to accept Freddy, or whatever he was, like, at face value. I was always wondering what was behind what he said. You just talked to him like he was an ordinary person asking us questions about regular stuff." Walter looked out the window. "I was, like, wow, what am I into? You know what I mean?"

"A lot of stuff I don't understand," she said. "A lot of what *you* say, I don't understand. Freddy was just a little bit farther out there."

"Yeah, he was."

Jez put her glass down. "I'm feeling steadier," she said. "I just needed to rub up against somebody, I guess." She laughed. "You know what I mean!"

"I do. I'm glad you called me. I said you were in my life now, and I'm comfortable with that. You do good work with your hands, and I admire that."

She picked up her glass and raised it in salute. "Let's do this again."

And she left.

Walter poured himself another tequila. He really did feel comfortable with Jezebel—in spite of her name. He could see why she and Freddy got along, because both of them, on the surface anyway, were *ordinary folks* in the best sense of that term. They didn't pretend to be anything other than themselves.

Freddy, of course, was anything but ordinary. Walter sensed an intellect under that Tennessee drawl, an intellect that had to be far beyond his own. *Far beyond the formerly living Freddy, either,* he thought.

Still, the aliens lacked something that even ordinary humans possess: a gut feeling about relationships. Culture, maybe. The comfort of living with others and sensing a commonality even with strangers. *Isn't that what the word alien means?*
Not all people have that sense of commonality, but when it's missing it usually reflects a life of experiences that hinder its growth. Some people grow up suspicious and fearful of others; some become angry or arrogant to protect themselves from people they see as different from themselves.

He wondered about the differences between the alien-as-Abigail and the alien-as-Freddy. Freddy seemed in control and curious, as though he were an anthropologist studying a distant species. Abigail was fearful, in a situation she didn't understand. In retrospect, she had seemed more human to Walter, struggling to cope with something gone wrong in the system.

They must have a system, too. A plan, for whatever objective. "Here to observe," they said. *Maybe a system that was breaking down, and they were—or are—looking for another system that might work for them.* Walter got up, a little unsteadily, and went down into his shop. There was nothing he would attempt down there in his present condition. He just wanted to look at his work, at the sturdy chair that awaited varnish, at the little end table that some other workman had made years ago, sure that some unknown person would find it suitable for their purposes, both of them probably now dead. The table still existed.

His fuzzy consciousness pondered, and an odd sense of satisfaction emerged: *They need something that we have, but they think they can get it just by asking questions, seeking data instead of the swirling cocktail of hormones and the layer upon layer of neurons humans have accumulated over eons.*

"Tell me about love," Freddy had asked. Turning toward the stairs, Walter laughed. Rumi must have asked the same thing, but he had that same cluster of cells in his primitive brainstem, and he asked only for the frosting, the end taste of wisdom, not data.

Walter went into his study and withdrew a vinyl record from its sleeve. His hands were now steady as he gently lowered the needle into the groove. *I should have told Freddy to listen to Brahms.*

For the next forty-five minutes, Walter listened. The tequila had worn off by then, leaving him in the thrall of Johannes Brahms, the Nineteenth-Century genius who had all but dominated the Romantic Era of music. *It took him nearly twenty years to create that First Symphony,* Walter thought. *Ha! "Tell me about love." There are millions of words about love, but just listen to* this *and know what it is.*

That night he dreamed about telling—not Freddy, but the intelligence that had inhabited Freddy—about love. "You said you reproduce by 'song'," he told it. "This is *song*—this is how our culture reproduces. Listen to Brahms, or Chopin, or Rachmaninov. This is the juice that flows from mind to mind, that reminds us forever of love and feeling!

He awoke feeling the dried traces of tears on his cheeks. For hours, he lay there thinking of Freddy and Jezebel and Abigail, and of alien beings who knew how to bring the dead back to life but didn't know what human life *means*. He thought about poor Abigail saying, "I wish I were Abigail."

What a mixed up bunch of idiots they are! We humans spend millions of dollars trying to create artificial intelligence in a computer that can think as good as we do, and here these creatures are doing whatever they are doing to learn how to be human—something that is far more than just intelligence.

Maybe time isn't the same to them as it is to us. Maybe to them a thousand years is like a day to us. A day on the moon is twenty-eight of our days. We've evolved over millions of years—could they do it in the blink of an eye?

"Makes one appreciate people more," he said aloud. He sighed, and got out of bed. In his bathrobe, he made a pot of coffee and sat down in his study, listening to music.

The Chopin nocturne brought tears to his eyes.

Five

Walter took in a deep breath of spring air as he set his paper cup on the sidewalk table and sat down next to it. There was little traffic in the street just then, and a number of pedestrians were investigating the shops that had just opened.

"Coffee is good," he said quietly to no one, and propped his iPad up on the table. Skimming the news headlines, he glanced up now and then to take in the scene.

Someone appeared at his side. Before he had time to look up at her, she placed a hand on an adjoining chair and asked, "May I?"

He nodded, and held onto his tablet to make sure it didn't get knocked off the table as she sat. When her face appeared in his field of vision, Walter's heart jumped.

She smiled. "Do I know you?" she asked.

"Uh—of course, Daniele," he stammered. "You're my ex-wife." He couldn't take his eyes off of hers.

There was a twinkle there, the same twinkle he remembered from so many years ago. Her hair was shorter, her clothing less flamboyant. But it was her.

"Is that why I'm here?" She almost laughed, as though she had no idea.

"How are you, Daniele?" He didn't know what to say.

"I'm well," she said gently.

He noticed a faint scar down her cheek. *That was a serious wound,* he thought. Aloud, he said, "It's been six years,"

"Has it?" That little half-laugh again. "I'm afraid I don't remember, but you seem familiar to me."

It took him a long moment to reply. "You have amnesia?"

"I think that's what you call it."

"What happened?" He wondered if it might be connected with the scar on her cheek.

"A long time ago—they've told me it was a couple of years," she said nonchalantly, "They said I fell down some stairs."

His mind whirling, he sipped from his now-cool coffee. "I'm going to have another cup of coffee," he said, getting out of his chair. "Can I get you one?"

"Thank you. Black." Her voice was the same, yet somehow different, as though she had become accustomed to speaking a different language.

As he stood in line to get the coffee, Walter thought about the Daniele he remembered. She now seemed changed—almost more grown up or something. Of course, it had been six years. *We all change over time.*

A little feeling nagged at him.

Walking back outside, he saw her differently, too. The way she held her head, perhaps, was why. *Or an actress, playing the part of Daniele in a stage play.*

But he smiled as he set the two cups down on the table. "You look good, Daniele," he said.

"Thank you." Her smile was almost the same. *Really good actress.*

And then it hit him. He suddenly felt weak. *Abigale. Freddy.* "You're . . ."

"I was called 'Daniele' before."

"Before your amnesia." He still couldn't say it.

"Yes."

They sat silently for a few minutes, sipping at their paper cups of coffee in the air of a spring morning. But it was a different spring morning that he felt now, distorted as it was with some kind of reality-unreality shift that he had difficulty navigating through.

The Hitchhiker

"Tell me about Daniele," she said quietly. "I don't remember."

"How did you find me?" he asked.

"I don't know. I felt *pulled here.*"

"Pulled here, from where?"

"Dallas. I was in Dallas."

Walter took a deep breath. "You don't remember me?"

"Tell me," she said.

"We were married," he said, trying to think of how to express what he was feeling.

"Here in this city?"

"Yes. We were married for twelve years. You left me for another man."

"To be with another man?" Her forehead was wrinkled with a struggle to understand. "Why?"

"I guess you got tired of me." Walter felt caught up in an old, not completely forgotten state of mind. Of bewilderment, of loss, of anger. "I felt like you had just turned me off—turned a switch. When you said good bye, you didn't even look me in the eye."

She was looking into his eyes now, with something like sadness, but a lack of understanding. "Why would I have done that?"

He thought of Abigale that night, struggling to understand him in the most obvious situations. Memories flooded his mind with the feeling of that woman suddenly straddling him in her apartment, following some ancient impulse that had little to do with him as a person—a human being—yet seeming skilled at the task at hand.

"You would never have done that," he said, and then suddenly aware of how little that would mean to her.

"Oh, that. I should have been embarrassed, shouldn't I?" She laughed.

The full force of it hit him. "You remember that." Walter nodded. "You're one of them."

She smiled. "You are still on guard."

He sighed deeply, and leaned back in his chair, as though to put this woman—this creature—into perspective. "You look like my wife—my former wife—and yet you are not her, are you?"

"Who am I?" she asked, sounding innocent.

"Not who," he answered, "What are you?"

"You said, one time, that you still loved me, after all those years."

He frowned, trying to remember. "I told that to Freddie, about my ex-wife."

Walter was sweating now. His heart was pounding. He knew what was going on, and yet he didn't. They were playing a game, and it seemed that she had no more idea of the game than he did. "You're here to observe, aren't you?"

She frowned. "Yes," she said finally. "You know that?"

"Why come to me?"

"I don't know." She lowered her head and looked into the small opening in the lid of her coffee, as though there might be an answer there among the brown bubbles turning cold. "I have a longing," she said slowly, and then looked up at him. "This human I inhabit—this former human—gives me feelings, impulses, half-memories . . . many of which are about you, now I recognize." She smiled. "When I first found you here just now, it was like I had been carried along in a breeze for a long time, and suddenly it became a solid thing, a thread, attached to you."

Walter was no longer sweating. In a way, he felt strong in this situation. This creature knew less about him than he did about her—or them.

"You don't understand emotional relationships, do you?" he asked, trying not to challenge her.

The Hitchhiker

"You loved her—this Daniele—didn't you?" She was meeting his gaze.

"Yes." He paused. "She's dead, isn't she?" He felt a slight tug in his midsection as he said it.

Daniele nodded.

"How much of her is still alive in you?"

"Most of her body," she said, pinching her arm. "She was healthy and strong. Her mind is almost infinitely complex. We're trying to make connections."

He smiled wryly. "I worked hard to try to understand her mind. In the end, I was unsuccessful."

"She broke off your relationship, you said."

He shrugged. "I guess she fell for another man."

"I thought humans were generally monogamous."

Walter had to smile. "So did I."

"You are very kind," she said.

Walter was caught by her words. "You—she—Abigale—said that, *just that way*, in her apartment."

Daniele smiled. "Did I?"

"Yes."

"What did it mean to you?" Her voice was honey.

Walter lowered his gaze to his hands. Then he looked up into her eyes. "I guess it took me by surprise," he said. "Abigail was so distant before that, as though she didn't see me at all and was only concerned by her feeling abandoned by the others. She was reaching out to me."

Daniele was silent for a moment, then: "I was new then. I didn't know what to expect."

He smiled. "You took a risk."

She cocked her head. "Yes, I did, didn't I? I had a sudden *feeling* about you." She smiled, and held her arms wide. "It was like a song, brewing somewhere. In you. In you and me. Something special."

He smiled, but said nothing, thinking. Then, "A song."

She nodded. "Does that make sense to you? I'm not sure I understand it."

Walter's hands were shaking.

"What is that?" she asked, indicating his hands.

"He sighed. "I don't' know. Something that comes from stress or uncertainty. An unintentional reflex."

"What does it tell you?"

"Christ, you sound like a therapist! I don't know. Let's see, I'm tense from this conversation because I don't know where it's heading."

"I'm only here to observe." She said it with a straight face, but her eyes were twinkling.

He managed a smile. "Unbelievable. You tell me that Daniele is dead, and yet there's something of her in you, in her body. In one way, it's horrible, but in another way I want to grasp what's left of her."

"I'm sorry." Her face was sad.

He looked up, surprised. "Where does that come from?"

Her eyebrows raised, echoing his question.

"I don't' know what you feel!" he exclaimed. "All of the conversations I've had with you—with Abigail, with Freddy—have left me with the understanding that you cannot grasp emotions like humans do. Do you know what that feels like, to be sorry?

She looked at him for a long time. Finally, she said, "Walter, we are learning. Yes, I feel—here—" She pointed to her chest. "I don't' know what it is yet. It's something that she felt."

Walter slumped in the chair. "I wonder," he said quietly, "if she felt sorry about us."

Daniele frowned thoughtfully. "I don't know," the alien said.

"You don't know grief," Walter said, and sighed.

"I'm feeling something here," she said, pointing again at her chest, "that comes from you." She took his hand and placed it on her breast. "Is that grief?"

Walter folded his arms on the table and put his head down and began to sob. He felt a hand on his shoulder.

"I'm sorry," she said softly.

Suddenly he needed her to be Daniele. Looking up into her face, barely registering the scar there, he saw the woman he had loved for twelve years—no, *eighteen years.*

A tear welled up in one of her eyes and slid down her cheek. Suddenly she stood back, a strange look on her face. "I have to go," she said, turning away.

"Wait!" he shouted to her. "Where are you going?"

"I'll find you again, Walter."

The memory of his hand, guided by hers, on her breast stayed with him for days. How much of Daniele remained in that body? In that mind?

He finally phoned Jez. "Thought you might be interested," he said. "They are back."

Jez waited. Then she asked, "Freddie?"

"No." Walter choked up and had a hard time speaking. "My ex-wife, Daniele."

"I don't get it."

"Only it's not her."

"You think . . ."

"I *know.*" Walter took a deep breath. "She just came up to me, in front of the Coffee Bean on Front Street. She said she couldn't remember who I was, but she came right up to *me.*"

"Your ex-wife." Jez didn't have many words.

"She admitted who she—what she was. She's the same as Freddie, the same as Abigail."

"Holy smokes." Jez paused. "She say what happened to your ex?"

Walter's voice caught. "She fell down some stairs."

Jez was quiet for a moment. "How you doin', Friend? You said you still loved her."

Walter took a moment to reply. "Lemme call you back," he said.

"Gotcha." Jez hung up.

The next day was Sunday, and Walter sat with a bottle of vodka and listened to Sibelius's Fifth. In the early evening, his phone rang. It was Daniele's phone calling. His heart pounding, he answered. "You still have her phone," he said.

"Your number is still in it," she replied.

His mind seemed scrambled. "Still," was all he could say.

"Can we talk?" It was undoubtedly Daniele's voice.

"You know where I live?"

"Yes."

Walter kept losing his place. *How could she know where I live?*

"Okay," he said finally. "Now?"

"Yes."

The doorbell sounded within minutes, startling him. *She must have been out front when she called.*

Her short hair and the scar on her cheek took him aback for a moment. "I don't know what to say," he said. He gestured toward a chair.

Daniele smiled, and Walter felt like crying.

"I'm sorry," she said. "This must be hard for you."

The Hitchhiker

He nearly shouted, *"How would you know?"* But he swallowed, took a deep breath, and said, "I haven't seen her in a long time."

"No."

"Why?" he started, then took another deep breath, "why do you have to look like her?"

"I'm here to observe," she said simply.

"Goddamn it! What's that mean?"

She smiled again, and waited until his breathing quieted. "You and Daniele had a close relationship."

"Yes," he said, his voice still high and strained. "We did have—and then she left!"

Daniele started to put a hand on his, but stopped. "Two days ago, when we first met," she said, "I was picking up things from you, and from her—I think—that I needed to study."

Walter stood and got the vodka bottle from the table, then collected two glasses from the breakfront. Setting them on the coffee table, he said, "I don't know about you, but I need this."

She smiled again. "Abigail drank vodka, didn't she?"

Quietly, "My god," was all he could say. He poured the liquor into both glasses. "You've come a long way from Abigail."

Momentarily, she seemed perplexed.

Downing the vodka in a single gulp, he set the glass down and for the first time, he smiled.

Daniele's brow smoothed out again. "You told Freddie—" and she paused, "that you still loved Daniele. What does that mean to you?"

The heat in his throat from the drink was beginning to wane, yielding to a warmth that flooded his consciousness. "I still love you, Daniele," he said quietly. "For a while I hated you, too."

She smiled. "That's why I come to you as her."

"To confuse me?"

"No," she said, "no. Just the opposite."

Neither of them spoke for a long time.

Then Daniele said, "I didn't stop loving you, Walter. I just couldn't face you."

"What was it—an airline pilot?"

"I think so," she said. "From what I can gather from her memories—and the feelings connected with them—Daniele never felt about him the way she felt about you."

"Then why did she leave?" Walter was trying hard to control his voice.

"I wonder that, too."

He slumped. "I guess I wasn't very exciting."

"Exciting? What does that mean?"

He had to smile. "One minute I'm looking at Daniele, and then I'm hearing somebody who never knew Daniele."

"Tell me about *exciting*." She spoke the word as if it were in Hungarian or something.

"Exciting is arousing, usually sexually. Something, or someone, who is exciting stimulates you, leaves you a little breathless, uncertain but—but *aroused* in some way."

"Abigail was aroused by you." She seemed somehow satisfied with the thought.

Walter's face colored slightly, but he grinned. "That's the idea," he said.

"Abigail found you exciting." She smiled back.

Walter poured another drink. Daniele watched him, then picked up her own glass and drank.

"I'm feeling something," she said after a moment. "Warm." She pointed to her throat.

"Alcohol does that," he said, still smiling. "Give it another minute and you'll feel something else."

Her eyebrows rose just a trifle.

"It relaxes you," he said. "Makes you loose."
"Loose. Not the same as excited?"
"No. But . . ." He took a moment to breathe deeply and let it out. "It's like you don't care so much about how other people see you."
Daniele shook her head.
"It's like," and he smiled, "you are more aware of what's going on in your own mind, er, body."
"Hormones."
It was his turn to feel confused. "Where did you hear about hormones?"
"I think you used the term explaining to Freddie."
He laughed out loud. "Oh, my god!"
Daniele smiled sweetly and looked down at her hands.
"Okay," he said, "right now, are you Daniele, or . . . "
One beautiful eyebrow went up an eighth of an inch. After a moment, she said, "I see what you mean."
"You're feeling it?"
"Hormones. Yes. And alcohol."
Walter slumped back. His face was sad.
She took a deep breath and let it out slowly. "I'm sorry, Walter, that you lost her."
His voice was husky with emotion. "It's like watching an old home movie of someone who has died."
"I suspect," she said, "that it's more than that. A home movie wouldn't be able to converse with you."
"No."
"But this is very important for me—for us."
Just for a second, Walter could see behind the Daniele façade. There was *something* there, something that was not Daniele. "You are . . . "
She nodded, her face showing sadness, a different sadness than his sorrow of a moment before. "I feel . . . "
"Compassion," he said, watching her eyes.
"Feeling other people's emotions."

"Yes."

She looked at him silently for a long time. Then she reached across the coffee table and took his hand. Very softly, she asked, "Walter, do you want to make love to Daniele, one last time?"

Startled, he drew back.

"Just her. Nobody else. Nothing else. Just you and Daniele."

Daniele sat and waited, her eyes never leaving his.

Walter breathed deeply several times. This was Daniele, the woman he had loved for as long as he could remember, facing him, offering herself to him. And it wasn't. It was an alien being in her skin, with her words, her expression, her love. No.

"No," he said. "Thank you. No. My body—my *soul*, it feels like—wants very much to feel Daniele against me again. But you're not Daniele, and I couldn't make love to you. I've passed up the chance for sex with several women since Daniele left, because *they weren't her*. What happened between Abigale and me was just sex, and it felt good for a few minutes, but then it felt awful. I've been ashamed ever since."

Daniele's face changed subtly, but she continued to hold his gaze.

"I wasn't a very good person that night," he said. "I should have left her at the emergency room, let the professionals take care of her. I should never have drunk that vodka. I was irresponsible. Maybe if we hadn't had sex I could have faced the young man—Michael—and helped him take care of her. But my shame made me have to escape."

"You kept saying that you didn't know what to do," the alien said quietly.

He shrugged. "I was completely dumbfounded."

"What does that have to do with Daniele?" the alien asked. "You said you still love her."

"I love her memory. You look like her, but you're not her." He burst into tears and turned away. "Go away!"

As he buried his face in a pillow, he heard her get up quietly and go out the door.

After a long time, he sat up and wiped his face, looking across the room at where she had sat. It was as if her ghost still sat there. He shook off the impression.

Walter became aware of something else, a thought that gradually put itself together in his mind. It seemed the alien had learned something, It was *feeling something* for Walter. Maybe it was compassion. In his first conversations with it as Freddy, it wanted to know about sex and procreation, and then it wanted to know about love. Now, it seemed, there was something more.

Compassion is a kind of love, an undemanding wish to give, to help. In the beginning of a relationship, sex is a motivator to tighten the bond, but the bond is the thing. Like he tried to tell Freddy, there's a part that gives and a part that takes. For a while, it's important that each one gives and takes more or less equally. Maybe he hadn't ever grown past the taking part with Daniele—that's why he suffered so much, and for so long.

When he was offered the gift—what the alien thought was what he wanted—his body responded almost automatically. It meant little to the alien.

Or maybe it did. Maybe, in Daniele's body, it was more than a gift. Maybe at that moment it was more than generosity. Maybe Walter had become more than just useful to its purposes. Perhaps the alien *felt what Walter was feeling*, and like a human, was responding with what it thought he needed.

Walter still struggled to keep them separate. Part of him still clung to Daniele, or the thought of Daniele, like clutching an old photograph. Daniele, animated by the alien, was not Daniele.

He put the vodka and the glasses away, and went downstairs to his shop. The odors of varnish and fresh cut wood returned him to himself, at least for now. Daniele was dead, and now he might be able to look to his future, instead of his past.

The Hitchhiker

Twenty Years On . . .

One

The faint notes of the nocturne carried through the incessant throb of the engines as Walter picked up the two brandies from the counter and turned toward the music. Each perfect note owned the ear for an instant—a warm raindrop touching an upturned face, recognizable in that instant and then immediately blending with a thousand others caressing the skin—each note forever tucked into memory creating with its mates a feeling of *rightness*. "She does love Chopin," he said quietly to himself.

The soft light in the lounge wrapped around him, and he found an empty seat, setting the two glasses on the little table in front of him. He caught her eye and was rewarded with a flick of smile. The nocturne continued.

This cruise was his reward to himself for decades of office boredom, but he forgot the open sea outside the walls of the lounge, instead sinking every day into luxurious upholstery to listen to her play the piano.

Several pairs of hands clapped softly when she finished the piece; then she placed her own hands into her lap for a moment. She nodded and smiled shyly in acknowledgment.

He picked up one of the glasses to salute her, and he patted the seat next to him.

She silently obeyed his gesture, gliding over to him.

"Your playing makes me want to live forever," he said.

"Thank you." She picked up one of the glasses and sipped.

"Will you have dinner with me later?" He asked.

She nodded, holding his eye.

The Hitchhiker

Walter was still basking in his retirement. At first, he had spent his days in his shop, sanding smooth curves of furniture. Then he went away on the Caribbean cruise that he had promised himself for years. He hadn't been prepared for the loneliness of watching a thousand other people laughing, talking and playing together. He was used to being alone, but always in the privacy of his cubicle or the comfort of his little woodworking shop. In the midst of crowded gaiety he missed intimacy.

Until Clara.

Their quiet conversations over dinner led eventually to soft nights in his room.

They sat under an umbrella, eating lunch. "I want to find another place to live," he told her. "Some place with a view, but still having a wood shop."

"You want water or mountains?" Clara had been holding his hand, and now squeezed it.

"Both would be great. Mostly I want some visual stimulation."

"Music?"

"Of course," he said. "A big room, a big sound system." He paused. "Maybe a piano."

Her eyebrows went up. "Do you play?"

He grinned and shook his head. "Maybe I'll learn."

"Sounds awesome."

He took her hand in both of his. "How would you like to help me find a place?"

Clara looked down. "I don't know," she said softly.

"I'm sorry." He chuckled. "I'm getting ahead of us, aren't I?"

"You like my playing," she said, her voice becoming sad. "We have different lives."

Still holding her hand, he said, "I've just begun a new life. I can live anywhere. I would like very much if we could at least see each other once in a while."

"But you don't know anything about me, besides my piano playing." She withdrew her hand.

"I know more than you think."

She looked into his eyes. "Do you?"

"Yes."

She continued to hold his gaze for a long time.

"Am I too needy?" He asked finally.

Dropping her eyes, she said, "I don't understand a lot about life. I've been pretty sheltered."

"Where's your family?"

She stood. "I have to get back to my piano."

They walked together back to the lounge. The other occupants had left.

Standing beside the piano, she looked up at him, "Both of my parents died," she said. "I don't know if I have any other family. I just play music."

He started to put an arm around her shoulders, then thought better of it. "You play music on cruise ships. That's all?"

She sat down at the piano and smiled. "Not much of a life, is it?"

He sighed. "I thought *my* life was pretty empty."

Turning toward him, she said, "But you seem so—so, *cosmopolitan.*" And she laughed.

Another couple entered the lounge. They looked around. "I thought somebody would be playing the piano here," one said.

Clara stood up. "That's me," she said. "I was just taking a break."

"Classical, right?"

Clara opened the piano. "Do you like Schumann?"

The woman laughed. "I don't know much about music. I think so."

Clara began to play.

The couple clapped when she finished the piece.

"That's Robert Schumann?" the woman asked.

Clara smiled. "Clara Schumann."

The man looked at the placard standing next to the piano. "Clara Schumann—that's you?"

Clara laughed. "No. I just happen to have the same name."

"Relative?"

She smiled. "Only by her music."

"Robert and Clara were husband and wife," Walter said. "A lot of people think she was the greater of the two."

Clara flashed him a smile. "My parents thought I should have a famous name, and they loved the Schumanns' works."

"That would be a lot to live up to," the man said.

She turned the smile on him. "Sometimes it is." And then she began another piece without opening the sheet music in front of her.

The ship was nearing its home port, and passengers were setting their luggage out in the hallways.

Walter and Clara sat at the bar, having "one last drink."

"I'm not ready to say goodbye," he said, looking into her eyes.

Clara laughed. "The next cruise leaves on Thursday," she said.

"Why don't you get off with me? We'll go house hunting."

She laughed again, but looked down at her hands. "Walter, . . ." she began, and looked up at him.

"I know," he said. "You don't have any reason to trust me."

"Yes I do."

"Can you take some time off this job, and we'll just travel a little bit together. And just maybe in the process find me a new home."

"I have a contract," she said, "but I suppose they can always find another musician."

"Then what?"

"I don't' know." She looked at him, tears welling up in her eyes. "I DON'T KNOW!"

Surprised, he put his hand on hers. "Hey," he said, "I get it. You're just not ready." He sighed deeply. "It's been so long since I have felt this way about anyone. I just don't want to lose you!"

She looked out of the large window near them. The coast was visible ahead. People were on deck, hurrying back and forth.

She turned back to face him. "All right," she said. "I have to tell my boss, and I have to pack my things."

Walter's heart leaped in his chest. "Okay, come on. I'll help you."

They stood and embraced, then hurried toward her room. At the door, she inserted her key in the lock and looked up at him. "You're very kind," she said, then went through the door.

Walter felt the hairs on the back of his neck move. Then he followed her in.

A little while later, they went down the gangway together, holding hands and grinning at each other.

When they had located their luggage on the dock, he said, "You stand guard here, and I'll take the shuttle to the parking lot. I'll be back in a few minutes."

The Hitchhiker

She was still standing by the luggage when he pulled up with his car.

Two

He stood on the veranda with a beer in his hand, looking out over the lake to the mountains beyond. A gentle breeze came in off the water, and he wondered if one of those little float planes could land and take off there. *Could save a couple of hour's drive if we had one,* he thought.

Chopin was drifting out from the living room, where Clara was practicing. He loved the music in the house, and he loved the way she played with such feeling.

Clara had little knowledge or interest in cooking, so Walter had taken charge of their meals. She was quite fastidious about the way their home looked, however, bringing in flowers and hanging new pictures on the walls occasionally. He spent time in his wood working shop while she practiced on the piano. The sound of the piano, when it was not drowned out by the machinery in his shop, gave Walter a lot of pleasure.

He'd bought the piano for her even before they moved into the house. "I want to learn to play, too," he had said, "but only if you have the patience."

She had smiled and kissed him. "I'd love to."

Occasionally, they invited friends in to listen to her play, and she enjoyed "performing," as she called it.

Living in such a rural area, they didn't have many neighbors, but had met most of them at the local pub that was the only business at the local crossroads. It was a congenial group, mostly professionals, and the juke box in the pub even played some popular classical music.

"I met Clara on an ocean cruise," he told the group once, "shortly after I retired, almost fifteen years ago. She was playing in one of those quiet little lounges on the ship that had a piano and a group of easy chairs. She played mostly Chopin and Schumann—both Robert's and Clara's."

He looked at Clara. "When I asked her name during a pause in her playing, she laughed and said that her parents had loved the original Clara Schumann's music so much they named their daughter after that famous composer."

"It just happened," Clara told them, "that I took to the piano from an early age. "Maybe it was their encouragement, as well as my name that drew me to the piano."

One of the wives looked at Walter. "You went on a cruise by yourself?" she asked.

"The cruise was my reward to myself for thirty years of dull office work," he responded, repeating what he'd told many others. "Some friends tried to get me to take a lady along with me, but female companionship always seemed to take more effort than it was worth."

"And then you met Clara." Everybody laughed.

"My first marriage was a long time before," he said. "I never thought I'd ever do that again."

He and Clara held each other's eyes for a long time, until somebody broke the spell by spilling their drink.

"Where are you from, originally?" someone asked Clara.

"I grew up in Vienna," she said.

"But you don't have any accent at all, that I can hear."

Clara blushed slightly. "I think I've forgotten all of my original language." She smiled shyly. "I've been an American almost as long as I can remember."

"You know, I never thought of that," Walter said. He looked at Clara. "You could pass for a Midwesterner any day of the week"

Another person asked, "Where did you live before you joined the cruise line and traveled the world?"

Clara paused and looked down at her hands. "Columbus, I think," she said.

"Columbus, Ohio, right? Couldn't be Columbus Georgia with that accent!" Everybody laughed.

Clara glanced nervously at Walter, then got up and went to the juke box. She played an old recording by José Iturbi, "Clair de Lune."

Three

"Yes. Thank you," said Clara to her phone as Walter came up the stairs from his wood shop.

When she disconnected, Walter asked, "What was that about?"

She smiled. "I'm going on another cruise. Do you want to come?"

"What?"

"My old boss from the cruise line just called and asked if I could fill in for the pianist he had scheduled on a cruise next week but they came down with the flu."

Walter frowned, and looked at the calendar on his phone. "I have a hematologist appointment on Wednesday," he said.

"Do you mind if I go without you?" Clara put a hand on his arm.

He grinned. "As if I could stop you."

"No, really, Walter," she said. "I want to play again, but not if you're against it. It's only a week."

"Where's the cruise?"

"It leaves from Houston on Saturday and goes down to Belize and back."

"Well, go, of course."

She embraced him. "I'll miss you, you know." Leaning her head back so that she could see his face, she said, "I remember how nice it was that time, to see you sitting there every day while I played."

As she sat in the dim lounge at the piano, Clara thought about the first time she had seen Walter. There was something about him that she had immediately felt drawn to.

Three times a day, she played for an hour all of her favorite pieces from Chopin and the two Schumanns. Once, someone asked her to play a Liszt etude. She responded, "I'm sorry, I don't play Liszt. He just doesn't fit my style."

Another woman in the lounge spoke up: "The other Clara Schumann wouldn't play him, either."

Clara smiled. "Maybe it's a family trait," she said.

The woman approached the piano. "I remember you," she said. "You used to be a concert pianist, a long time ago, weren't you?"

"When I was young," Clara answered, and began to play.

After the piece, the woman spoke again. "I heard that you had been killed in an automobile accident. Was that not you?"

Clara laughed. "Obviously, I didn't die, did I? I was badly injured, and I had to retire from the concert circuit."

"You were good, though. I still have a recording you made with the Rochester Orchestra."

"That was a long time ago," Clara said.

The woman smiled. "I'm glad you're still playing."

"Thank you."

At Clara's last scheduled appearance in the lounge before their return to Houston, the woman appeared briefly and left her a generous tip.

On the airplane back home, she thought about those years after the accident and how difficult it had been to learn to play all over again. About the accident itself, she had no memory. Her hands, she found, remembered.

Her reunion with Walter gave her profound joy.

Four

Walter was not well. The hematologist told him that his bone marrow was not replenishing his blood well enough, and they scheduled a series of transfusions.

Clara learned to cook and help him bathe, and the two of them grew even closer as time went on. When he felt well enough to work in his wood shop, he managed to finish a cherry desk chair that he had begun years before but had set aside in order to make other furniture for their home.

After some months, it was apparent to both of them that Walter's time was near. Clara sat by his bedside every day, or went into the living room to play for him.

"Clara," he said quietly one day, "promise me something?"

"Of course, my love."

"Don't let them take me."

She looked at him quickly. "What do you mean?"

"You know," he said, managing a weak smile.

Clara burst into tears, and buried her face in the pillow next to him. He reached up and patted her shoulder.

"How long have you known?" she asked softly.

"Long time," he answered. "It was years after we got together, and there were little clues, every once in a while." He looked into her eyes. "Once—I don't remember when—you said something to me, 'You are very kind,' and I flashed on those words, spoken in that exact way, from before we knew each other. Do you remember?"

"Of course."

"You have learned a lot about being human," he said. "When I began to realize who you were, I didn't want to admit it to myself. I didn't want to admit it to you. By that time I loved you too much. If it was all a sham, I was willing to live the sham with you."

She sat up and took his hand in hers. "My love was—my love is—not a sham," she said. "You have taught me so much about what it is to be human."

"Even before we met, you had learned a lot," he said. "I didn't guess, for a long time. By the time I felt sure, it was okay. I still loved you, whatever that means."

"Just now you asked me to promise you."

"Yes. I've had a good life. I can't imagine living without you—my Clara. You don't need my body."

"Clara can't imagine living without you, either," the alien said, holding his gaze.

He looked out the window. "I'm impressed," he said, his voice husky, "how you were able to pick up her piano talent. You play so wonderfully," and he looked back into her eyes, "so full of feeling."

"We talked, you and I, a long time ago, about our songs." She stroked his forehead gently.

"I remember," he said, smiling.

"You are dying soon."

"Yes."

"So will Clara." She held his gaze. "She will lie down with you and she will leave with you."

"I love you," he managed to say, and closed his eyes.

Clara Schumann lay down beside him.

The song remained.

The End

The Troubadour

One

♪ *Are the stars out tonight?* ♪

You could barely hear the throaty baritone through the noise in the restaurant. Kathryn smiled as she touched the glass to her lips.
"He sounds like Bing Crosby," I said.

♪ *I don't know if it's cloudy or bright* ♪

"I was thinking Perry Como," she replied.
I turned to watch the singer strolling among the tables with what looked like a mandolin. Dressed in all black, he had dark hair, a mustache and a sporty goatee. A white towel hung from his belt.
Turning back to her, I grinned, and she responded in kind. "I heard he's the kid brother of the owner," she said.
"Where'd he pick up that song?"
"Probably from late-night TV."

♪ *Cause I only have eyes for you, Dear.* ♪

Kathryn sipped her cosmopolitan.
I pointed at her glass. "It goes with your drink," I said.
"Next he'll sing 'Moonlight Becomes You'."
I managed to half-sing, "It goes with your hair."
She chuckled. "He certainly knows the right thing to wear." Her singing was better than mine.

We both turned to watch the singer, until our waitperson arrived with our salads. "You like the singing?" the woman asked as she prepared the table.

"He's got a good voice, but you can hardly hear him in this room," Kathryn said.

"I heard he's been trained professionally." The waitperson straightened up and looked over at the singer. "His brother owns the place."

"Yes."

She held the cheese grinder over Kathryn's salad. "Parmesan?"

Kathryn and I both nodded.

After she had left us, I said, "That's a mandolin, isn't it?"

"I don't think he's been playing it. I can't hear it, anyway."

I laughed. "Maybe just a prop, like his outfit."

Between bites, we watched the singer make his way among the tables on the far side of the room. He stopped now and then to chat and laugh with customers.

"If he comes over here, will you request a number?" I asked.

Kathryn smiled. "Hmm. Yes. 'You Go to My Head.' Frank Sinatra."

I watched her as she ate.

Kathryn was tall, and at one time had been a knockout. Now, still beautiful, she still wore her light brown hair long like the young girls do these days. Just a hint of gray showed over her temples when she fingered it back over her ears. Her clothes tended toward the flashy, and her nails were bright red.

She and I had known each other many years ago, having met in college when I had the idea that I wanted to be a writer. She majored in English composition at first, but then changed to business school and went on to get an MBA. We'd lost track of each other until a recent cocktail party, where she stood, as I had always remembered her, in the center of a circle of men. Later, when I found her standing alone at the bar, I greeted her and we embraced.

"So good to see you!" she gushed.

"You look great."

"Thank you. You do, too."

We found a couple of chairs together at the side of the room and accounted for the nearly thirty years since we'd last seen each other—the highlights, anyway. I'd been married and divorced, like most people I knew. She ticked off the names of four husbands, three of whom were "ex" and the fourth was currently overseas working a large business deal.

"I manage a little fund over on Charles Place," she said, smiling and sipping her martini.

"You had a head for business, even back in school."

"It's very competitive," she said, pulling her mouth to one side, as if she were relating a confidence.

We had agreed to have dinner together, "for old time's sake."

Now, in the dimly-lighted restaurant, Kathryn's beauty was shown off to her advantage. Although we had slept together a couple of times in college, neither of us had been interested in a long-term relationship. In particular, I had always been aware that

I'd have to contend with her self-centered way of attracting males.

"Even in the eighties you went for Frank Sinatra," I said.

"Michael Bolton and Michael Jackson just didn't do it for me." She smiled. "I wanted a grown-up man."

"So tell me about your present husband. Grown up?"

"Very." She tilted her cosmopolitan glass and looked in it.

"Another?" I was ready to signal the waitperson.

"No, but I'll have wine with my Chicken Parmesan." Looking up at me, she said, "He's older. Mature."

"Happy?"

"Yes. We have lives that separate us occasionally, like now, but we're solid."

The singing waiter appeared at our table, singing something I didn't recognize and strumming on the mandolin. Kathryn looked up at him and smiled. "Joe Jackson," she said.

He let the mandolin dangle at his side. "You aren't that old," he said in that rich baritone.

She laughed. "You are smooth! I had all of his CDs."

"As a child, of course." He winked at her. "Have something special you want to hear?" The look on his face spoke another kind of invitation.

"Something from before you were born—'You Go to My Head'?" It was a dare.

He picked up the instrument and played a little intro before launching into the song. He played well.

> ♪ *You go to my head,*
> *And you linger like a haunting refrain*
> *And I find you spinning round in my brain*
> *Like the bubbles in a glass of champagne* ♪

Electricity was sparking between them. I sat there watching Kathryn glow in his attention. He sang with a slight smile on his face, totally aware of her, playing her just as he was playing his mandolin. I was embarrassed to be witnessing the whole thing, feeling the stares of people around us.

When he finished singing, he added a little flourish with the instrument and then bowed slightly to her.

She clapped softly, her eyes on his all the while. "Thank you," she whispered.

"A Billie Holiday number," he replied.

I started to hand him a five, but he waved it away. He nodded to me and said quietly to Kathryn, "M'Lady", then moved on.

I waited until her eyes left his back and returned to me, then said simply, "Wow."

She grinned. "He's good, isn't he?"

"In more ways than one."

Then she looked down sheepishly. "Was it that obvious?"

I looked to one side, scratched my head and smiled.

Just then the waitperson reappeared. She grinned at us. "I waited, but I was afraid your dinners were getting cold."

Kathryn took a deep breath and let it out.

"Can I get you anything else?" the woman asked as she took away our salad plates and set our entrees down.

"A nice cab," said Kathryn, smiling at her.

"Make it two," I added, feeling rather superfluous at the moment.

"You got it."

When she left, I said to Kathryn, "I have never seen you quite so—captured."

She laughed and busily buttered a dinner roll.

"And I've only seen you blush once before." I was beginning to enjoy this.

She looked up at me, her face questioning, then brightened. She laughed again. "When you first propositioned me."

"You remember too?"

Quietly, "Of course, Richard. You were my first."

"It's been thirty years," I said.

"And hundreds of other men." She had an impish grin on her face. To my raised eyebrows, she added, "well, maybe not hundreds."

"At least four."

"At least four."

"It was special," I said.

She smiled slightly. "You weren't a virgin."

"I'm glad."

"So am I. I was then, too."

I sighed. "Oh, Kathy." My words were drawn out.

We gazed into each other's eyes for a long time.

"Your dinner is getting cold," she murmured.

We hadn't seen each other for a couple of weeks, when she texted me:

| Free for another dinner at *Impetuoso* tonight? |

| Sure |

| Pick me up at 7. You know where I live? |

| Of course |

| ♥ |

She was waiting for me at her door when I pulled up. She wore a white dress with a very low-cut neckline, and a tiny whale-tail pendant.

"I called for reservations, but they said you'd already done that," I said as she got into the car.

She turned her head toward me and looked down. She seemed not to know what to say, but finally blurted, "I hope you don't hate me, Richard. You were my second choice tonight."

A small tug at my midsection. "I'm happy for crumbs."

"Oh! Don't say that! It wasn't like that. I shouldn't have said that." She put a hand on my arm and her eyes pleaded with me.

I laughed. "Kathryn, how long have we known each other?"

She seemed genuinely remorseful. "It was an old friend—female. I wanted to show off my troubadour."

Have you been back there since we were there?"

She smiled sheepishly. "Last weekend." Then, seeing the look on my face, she added, "He's as good as he looks."

"Uh, I guess I won't ask." I was beginning to wonder what our dinner this evening was going to be like. Watching them flirt with each other a couple of weeks ago was mildly entertaining, but I wasn't sure I wanted to sit there while they drooled at each other.

Besides, I thought, what am I doing there? I'm not a chaperone, certainly. A shill, to distract others from the obvious romancing that was going on?

I had to admit to myself that I was just a little jealous. Since she and I had met again after all those years, I'd been remembering how much I had enjoyed her coquetry back in college, especially when it was directed at me. And after she got the hang of it, her love making was memorable.

The Troubadour

It didn't take long after we had settled into our cocktails before the singer appeared again. He had upgraded his performances with the addition of wireless mics, both on his lapel and his mandolin. Now, as he cruised the tables on the other side of the restaurant, his songs carried all over the room.

♪ *Fly me to the moon, and let me play among the stars...*

I grinned at Kathryn. "He knows you like Sinatra."
"Maybe," she said with a smile.
"Does he sing to you in bed?" I immediately regretted saying it.
She didn't answer, looking down at her menu.
"I'm sorry," I said. "That was gauche."
When she looked up at me, her eyes were serious.
"I'm sorry," I said again.
"You think I'm a slut?"
"No."
"I'm not sure I believe you."
I took a breath and let it out slowly. "Kathy, I've never judged you. You've always enjoyed playing with men."
"I used to look up to you."
"Yes, I know you did."
"You used to encourage me to play."
"It was part of your charm."

♪ *I've got you under my skin...* ♪

With the enhancement of the audio system, he really did sound a lot like Frank Sinatra. I saw Kathryn look up, and her troubadour appeared at our table.

♪ *I've got you deep in the heart of me...* ♪

She looked up at him and smiled, but I could tell she didn't want to deal with him right then.

He registered the change, and moved on, still singing.

♪ *So deep in my heart that you're really a part of me...*

"I'm sorry, Kathy. I've spoiled it, haven't I?"

"I want to leave," she said softly. "Please take me home."

I hesitated for only a moment, then stood up. "Okay."

The waitperson came to us immediately, and I handed her my credit card. She started to say something, then looked at Kathryn and nodded to me.

In the car, I touched the start button, and then turned to her. "Kathy—" I began.

"Richard, I'm not that person anymore," she said, her voice low and tight. She was looking straight ahead.

"Who was that person, Kathy?"

"I don't know." She turned to face me. "Who were you then?"

I sighed. "I don't know. I didn't know then."

We sat in silence for a long time. I thought of starting the car, but waited. There was something we needed to get through, something left over from thirty years ago that we didn't deal with at the time. Something I hadn't thought about in all those years.

Two

We had been in several freshman classes together, and I noticed her right away. Tall and gorgeous, she attracted the stares of male students wherever she went. She was shy, however, and some of the guys obviously intimidated her. I wasn't pushy, thinking of her like a bird, always on tiptoes, ready to fly away.

After a few weeks we began smiling at each other. It was probably during the class in Shakespeare Sonnets that we actually started talking to each other. The hints of passion in the poems stimulated my thoughts of her. She, however, expressed concern during class discussions that physical love seemed to carry the threat of hurt. My little bird perched tentatively on its branch.

At the end of the first quarter, we compared our schedules, and agreed to meet for cokes following a Friday afternoon class we were both in. That became a regular thing, and soon we were having dinner together, sharing our class notes.

We ended up in bed together in her dorm room one weekend after her roommate had gone home.

"Kathy," I said, after it was over, "talk to me."

She lay there, tears streaming down her cheeks, her eyes closed.

"Did I hurt you?" I wiped her cheek with my fingertips, feeling terrible, as though I had ruined everything between us.

She opened her eyes but stared at the ceiling. "A little," she said softly, "at first."

"I'm sorry."

She turned her head toward me, a slight smile forming. "You were wonderful. I was just scared."

It had happened suddenly for both of us. We'd gone from laughing and kissing to clinging desperately to each other, and then all I could think about was how much I wanted to be inside her. She hadn't resisted me, but neither had she opened herself to me. All through it, her body had been as tense as a coiled spring.

"I'm sorry," I said again, "I didn't want it to happen like that. I just lost myself." I felt my own tears come as I buried my face in her soft neck. She stroked my hair.

Later, we were both quiet as we dressed and left her dorm room. I kept looking around, wondering if anybody could tell what we had been doing. The hallway was empty.

At the entrance to her dorm, we kissed tentatively and I went back to my room.

That night in my own bed, I was eager for more of her.

I had dated during high school, and lost my virginity during the summer between my junior and senior years. The girl was much more experienced than I. Entering college, I thought I was sophisticated. It didn't take me long to discover how much I didn't know about girls. There were those who saw sex as adventure, and those who seemed to think it was a rather distasteful chore, to be endured for the sake of a relationship.

Kathryn was not one of them. What she lacked in experience, it seemed, she made up for in enthusiasm.

The next time I saw her in class, she looked at me differently, as though we shared a secret. Mike, a friend who happened to be standing next to me, saw this and poked me in the side without saying anything. I didn't look at him, but I knew he was grinning. Kathryn seemed not to notice.

At lunch, she touched my hand across the table, then withdrew.

"How are you?" I asked.

She simply smiled. We had passed some kind of milestone in our relationship. At that point, I was feeling just as warm.

"There doesn't seem to be anything to say," I began, "like words don't mean enough."

"I never knew," she said.

We didn't have another opportunity for sex until her roommate went home for the weekend again several weeks later. In the meantime, I had been thinking about Kathryn almost constantly. We didn't talk about it when we spent time together, but it was always there in the background of our conversations. We shared notes and discussed the current topics of our classes. Our hands touched a lot.

When I was not with her, a niggling concern nudged my consciousness: the future. I had decided when I entered college that I would not become serious about a girl until I finished my degree. Because we were not talking about our relationship, I wondered if she had any expectations.

In our early conversations, I had spoken of my intention to not get serious about anybody. She seemed to understand and agree. "I have to focus on my studies," she said. "It's too hard to try to juggle my time as it is."

The way she looked at me after our night together made me nervous.

So when we again found ourselves alone in her room, it felt different. I was less aroused. She probably picked up on that, and seemed shy again. We made love, but the afterglow wasn't the same.

"Richard, what's wrong?" she asked, her eyes serious.

I confessed that I had been wondering if our making love had changed something in our relationship.

"Of course it did. How could it not?"

"I mean," I tried to explain, "I thought we had agreed that neither of us wanted a commitment until we were out of college." It felt lame to me as I said it.

Her eyes changed. "Do you mean that you want to have sex with others?"

I tried to find words. "No," I mumbled finally.

"Then what?" She was sitting up in the bed, clutching the sheet in front of her. "I don't want to be just one of your interchangeable bedmates."

"That's not what I mean at all," I protested. "I don't know what this means for the future."

She held out her left hand. "There's no ring on this finger, is there?" Her eyes were on mine, and they weren't friendly.

I shook my head.

"Did I say I wanted one?" The softness was gone from her voice, as well.

"I'm sorry," I said, wishing I could turn the clock back.

She got out of bed and began dressing, her back to me. My gut felt as though someone had punched me. I put my clothes on as she retreated to the bathroom.

The next week was terrible for me. Kathryn and I didn't speak and didn't keep our regular times together. When our eyes met, which was only occasional, hers felt cold to me.

"The thrill is gone." Mike, my friend who had sensed when Kathryn and I had first made love, put his hand on my shoulder as we walked down the crowded hallway.

I gave him a wry smile.

He threw his backpack onto his shoulder and stuck out his left hand, wiggling his fingers.

I shook my head.

He looked around at the students walking with us down the hall. "Even if she doesn't ask for it, that's what she wants," he said out of the corner of his mouth.

"No," I replied. "She said she's not looking for anything like that."

A resigned, "Yeah, man."

We turned into the lunchroom, and didn't say anything until we had gotten our cokes and chips and found a table away from the crowd.

"I was just feeling a little trapped, I guess," I said. "Not anything she said. But when I said it, she got pissed."

He nodded. "Guilty conscience."

"What d'you mean?"

"I mean that you're feeling guilty about the sex 'cause you think you ought to give her a ring—or a promise, at least."

I laughed. "You know, right after that first time, I thought it'd be nice to give her something."

"So what'd she say? 'Never in a million years!'?"

"Not quite."

He laughed. "Man, do you have a lot to learn about women!"

After a while, Kathryn and I began to connect again, even having dinner together late in the quarter. That's when she told me she was changing her major.

We never made love again. After a while, both of us began dating other people. She seemed to have a lot of new friends.

That was a long time ago.

Three

I phoned her again the next Monday evening. She was home, she said, catching up on her reading. "I hope I didn't spoil your evening," she said.

"I thought I had spoiled yours."

"Can you come over some evening this week?" she asked. "I'd like to clear the air, if we can."

"Sure. Tomorrow?"

"How about Wednesday? Come after dinner—I don't want to make too much of it."

I'd been thinking about the past as I pulled up in front of her condo. Kathryn had reacted strongly that long-ago time in her room in college, and had been just as quick to anger the other evening. Both times, after I had said something wrong. Was it just me?

She greeted me warmly, as she had done when we first reconnected at the cocktail party. She was wearing loose, flowing pajamas and slippers, her hair pulled back with a comb. "Glass of wine?" she asked.

"Sure—whatever you're having."

She brought out a bottle of red. "This is Argentine," she said as she poured. "I like it a lot."

"Super."

We sat opposite each other across the coffee table, and were silent for a short while.

Finally, I said, "Kathy, I hope you'll forgive my gaff the other night. I was just flip. I really don't know you well enough after all these years to make remarks like that."

She smiled. "I was not in a very good place that evening. I had been planning to have dinner with an old friend, and she had put me off at the last minute."

"You said I was second choice."

"Oh, Richard, I wish I hadn't said that!" She gave a little embarrassed laugh and put her glass down. "That was thoughtless."

"I'll admit, it took me aback a little."

"Back—to what?" She tilted her head, watching me.

"No, I don't mean back to the past." I laughed. "I mean I just didn't know how to respond."

"As I remember, you parried the remark very well. Something about crumbs."

I hung my head and laughed again. "What we have here..." I began.

"Is a failure to communicate! Yes—I remember that film."

We both laughed.

She took a sip of wine. "I promise, I won't shoot you."

"I don't make a very good Cool Hand Luke," I said.

She smiled. "You've always been as good as Paul Newman."

"Wow. I consider that a compliment."

"That's what I intended."

I looked at her, this middle-aged beauty that I had passed up thirty years ago. She was poised now, easy to laugh, sophisticated. I wondered what it would have been like to spend all those years with her.

"So," I said, "you invited me over, you said, to clear the air."

"I hope that's what we are doing."

"I'm all for that. Maybe we both put our foot in our mouth sometimes. Is the problem just between us?"

She smiled. "I wonder. I don't usually do that—at least I don't think I do."

"I got to wondering, the other night, if we might have something unfinished between us from thirty years ago."

She patted the sofa next to her. "Come sit over here," she said. "You're too far away for this conversation."

I did as she said, and she turned her body to face me, tucking a bare foot under her. "I spend my days strategizing about finances." She took a sip of wine and put the glass down. "I'm aware that I need other kinds of experiences."

I thought about her troubadour, but didn't say it. Instead I said, "You seem really comfortable with people."

"Not nerdy?"

"Far from it."

"Thank you. There is a soft side of me."

I started to speak, then stopped.

"What?" Her eyes widened a little.

"I well remember that soft side of you."

"Cool Hand Luke." She showed a sly smile.

"Really, Kathy."

"Do we need to talk about that night?"

"I don't know. Thirty years ago?"

"Richard." She paused. "I want you to kiss me first—then we can talk."

I did, holding it a long time, until I felt her relax the slightest bit.

When we parted, we both picked up our wine glasses.

Her voice was several tones lower when she spoke. "Tell me what you remember from that night."

I guess I looked down, for she said, "Richard, look at me."

"I think I was scared," I said.

"Of me?"

"No. I guess of the consequences. The possible consequences."

She frowned. "I'm sure you used a condom."

I shook my head and laughed. "No, it wasn't that. I just thought that we had gone through some kind of portal. Like, I had—at least I thought I had—my life all planned out."

Kathryn sighed. "It's hard to remember, isn't it? Thirty years ago, we were *so young!*"

"Okay," I said, "tell me how you remembered that night."

She took a deep breath and let it out. And then she took another sip of wine. "I had been afraid of sex, especially the first time. There was so much stuff I'd been told, about the pain and the bleeding, and feeling helpless. I didn't have any of that."

"You told me it had hurt a little."

She smiled at me. "Yes, it hurt a little, but not what I was expecting."

I waited for her to continue.

"When it was over, I felt this, this *euphoria*! I thought, 'Why did I wait so long?'" She put her hand on mine. "I loved you so much at that moment."

After a moment, I said, "And then I spoiled it for you."

Kathryn held my eyes. "The next time, it was as if I was feeling everything, and you were just feeling trapped."

I emptied my glass and set it down. I couldn't look at her. "A few years after that," I said, "I was at a Greek wedding, a friend of mine. The best man was the groom's older brother. I don't know what his circumstance was, but in the middle of the ceremony, he passed out cold. Right there in front of everybody."

"My goodness!"

"I thought at the time that he was terrified of the whole thing, even though he wasn't the one getting married. And, oh, I forgot—everybody was so serious there. They're like Catholics, the ceremony is pretty solemn. But when the bride came down the aisle, she had this huge grin on her face, the whole way down."

Kathryn snorted. "And to you, marriage really is getting trapped?"

"Is that why men have this reputation for being afraid of commitment?"

She had a smile on her face. "I don't know. Do you?"

"What, do I know why men have the reputation, or do I have a fear of commitment myself?"

She shrugged. "Does the shoe fit?"

"I don't know. Thirty years ago? I was a kid, looking forward to a lifetime. I thought I had it all figured out."

"Do you know what I was feeling then?"

I poured more wine in both our glasses.

"I was feeling, 'What fun!' I had never experienced anything like it. I had no desire for commitment. I wanted the freedom of romance."

I nodded. "You did seem to change, after we broke up."

She grinned. "The boys in the English department were so *serious*. That's why I changed majors."

I felt deflated. After a long silence, I asked, "Then why did you get upset with me the other night?"

She turned and looked down at her glass. Taking a large sip, she carefully set the glass back on the table. Without looking at me, she said quietly, "That first time? I was blown away by it—by you. I'd have—yes, I'd have married you in a minute right then if you'd asked me. You were so gentle with me, so loving. I'd been expecting sweaty bodies wrestling on the bed, and you made such sweet love to me!"

Tears streamed down her cheeks. She laid her head on my shoulder, and I wrapped my arms around her.

After a long time, she straightened up and wiped her face with a tissue. Looking up at me, she said, "All these years, I've remembered that first night. There has never been another night like that—" She smiled. "In thirty years."

My throat felt constricted as I tried to speak. "Then what was the other night about?"

"I've had you on this pedestal, and I thought you were judging me. I felt crushed."

"It was a crude remark. I think I was jealous of that guy. Maybe it *was* a dig."

Kathryn smiled sweetly at me. "You were jealous?"

I nodded. "Yeah."

"I could make love to you right now!" Before I could react, she put both hands up between us. "That would be a mistake. We're here to clarify things, not complicate them."

"Thank you," I said, "I wouldn't want that right now either."

She smiled. "Since we reconnected at that party, I've thought about you, and about when we were young. I know that both of us must have changed a lot in thirty years. In my head," she said as she touched her forehead, "I've carried you as you were then—no, maybe not as you were but as I saw you then."

She took my hand in hers. "You couldn't know how much you meant to me." Looking down, she went on, "and when you pulled away from me, I couldn't handle it. We were never the same after that."

I sighed. "Too bad we didn't go for counseling."

That brought a chuckle from both of us.

I played with my glass on the table. "You changed."

"How?"

"At first, you just seemed to open up to me. It was like heaven!"

"And then?"

"It was like you were a different person. You became more open to everybody. You flirted with guys, you had these happy conversations with people. I didn't know who you were." I turned to face her. "Before, I had this image of you as a fragile little bird, so vulnerable, so fearful—and then all of a sudden you were…"

"What, a hawk?" She was half-smiling.

"No! I don't know!"

"I discovered something about myself," she said, "I stopped being afraid. I felt like I knew something I hadn't known before."

I leaned back in the sofa. "You found your power?"

She stopped and looked at me. "Yes."

"Beauty is power."

"Not just beauty. Yes, I've known that. But something else. I suddenly knew the rules of the game."

"So you went into business and finance."

She smiled. "Business is a power game."

We stopped and sipped our wine.

"Your flirting with your troubadour?"

"A different kind of game. But yes." She leaned back. "Men are such babies." Then she looked over at me. "Not you."

"Maybe."

She grinned broadly. "He did sing to me in bed," she said.

"Ouch."

"I'm sorry, Richard. I was playing, like you said."

I got up and moved toward the door. "That was pretty clear," I said, turning as I reached the door.

She leaped off the sofa and came toward me. "Don't leave it here," she said, reaching a hand toward me.

I took her hand. "Okay," I said, "we need to continue. But right now I need to process."

"Call me—please?"

"I will."

I went home wondering why Kathryn, after all these years, affected me so much. She was not my first love, and certainly not my last.

The Troubadour

Six years ago my wife and I decided to separate, simply because we had taken such different paths in our lives. Without children to bind us together, we had found ourselves spending less and less time together. Neither of us had had an affair, but I found myself looking at other women. We sat down one night and had a long, respectful, conversation.

Afterward, our mutual friends didn't feel they had to choose between us, and we often found ourselves at the same gatherings. Once, about a year after our divorce, we got smashed at a party and went home to her apartment for the night. It didn't change anything.

Until now, my memories of Kathryn had been dim but pleasant, a scrapbook of faded photographs. I assumed that she went on with her life as I had, and that we'd probably not see each other again.

Now, she was vivid in my thoughts. And troubling. I pictured her the way I had found her several weeks ago at that cocktail party, in the middle of a circle of men, laughing and flirting.

Four

We had agreed to continue, but there was no time line, no date to get together. I wanted some space, some time to forget the past again, to restore the fading scrapbook of memories to its place on the shelf.

I called Sally, another friend, a poet with whom I had spent several weekends on the Carolina coast, watching sea birds and writing. "Have an evening free for dinner?"

"Of course, Richard," she said. "This weekend?"

"Found an interesting restaurant over on the other side of town." *Ugh,* I thought. *What was I thinking?* But I went through with it.

When the "singing waiter" came in that evening, he was doing songs from the eighties, like Lionel Richie's "All Night Long."

♪ *Everybody sing, everybody dance ...*
Lose yourself in wild romance, ... ♪

I was disappointed, but Sally enjoyed it. "He's got a good voice," she said, "but he doesn't sound like Lionel Richie."

Why was I disappointed? I remembered Kathryn remarking about the singers from the eighties and their high-pitched voices. "I want a grown-up man," she had said.

"The last time I was here," I told Sally, "he was singing the old Sinatra classics." I didn't suggest that she request a song when he came by our table.

When he did come around, Sally waited until he was out of earshot, then laughed and murmured, "He's kind of creepy looking, with that little beard."

The Troubadour

We drank white wine with our antipasto and carbonara. Sally is usually pretty quiet, although after a few glasses of wine she loosened up. I forgot Kathryn for the evening.

Following the meal, I took her to my place and made Spanish Coffees for us while we watched a foreign film on television. We both fell asleep on the sofa before it ended, and it was three A.M. when I finally took her home.

Sally was a comfortable friend. Never having been married, she was content with her life, and often took trips by herself, usually to quiet places and retreats that asked little of her. She'd published a couple of small books of poetry through specialty publishers. We had met at one of her readings in a book store that has since gone out of business.

My own writing seemed to have hit a snag. (I pictured that word as it is usually applied to a broken branch of a tree partly hidden under the surface of a river, waiting for something to come along with the current, ready to capture it. I imagined a leaf, caught in its travel, wiggling to free itself, depending upon some random force to come along and allow it to continue—to what end? Where does a floating leaf hope to go?)

I texted Sally so that someone would know where I'd gone, and drove down to the North Carolina coast. Sitting on the steps of the cabin that she and I had sometimes rented, I watched the surf and the birds and drank myself into a stupor.

I tried to remember what it felt like when I finally married Susanna, so many years ago. Did I have those doubts about a future with her, doubts that loomed so much with Kathy? We had a lot of good years together, with her teaching school and sometimes supporting me until I published my first novel. After that, I paid her back by cooking and keeping our home while she fussed with course booklets and grading papers. At the end she said that she wanted to be with someone who took a more active part in the world. I was immersed in fictional characters who, if they didn't actually do my bidding, didn't judge me.

 Opening my laptop the morning after I arrived, I tried to find out where my characters had gone. Finally I put them away and began a new story. Surprisingly, it flowed like a mountain stream.

A couple of days later I realized that I was rewriting history—the history of Kathryn and me. I had an impulse to call her right then. We had agreed to continue our conversation from that evening. Was that conversation also nothing but rewriting history?

How can one remember accurately after thirty years, recapture those feelings that altered the course of our lives? It's easy to say that one develops perspective over the years and can see more clearly the issues and the events of youth. Maybe not.

Were the feelings I had that first night back again with Kathryn, listening to her troubadour sing love songs to her—were they anything like the feelings I had for her when our relationship fell apart like the cake in the rain at MacArthur Park?

♪ *And I'll never find that recipe again*
Oh, no... ♪

Maybe all of my stories are history rewritten, maybe even the same history, cloaked in costumes and settings to hide them from myself.

I read over what I had just written. Maybe this time I should finish the story and just give it to Kathy. I didn't know if she'd understand it or not. Maybe my stories are more honest than I am, face to face.

The End

---

[i] "Both Sides Now" written by Joni Mitchell
[ii] "Send in the Clowns" written by Stephen Sondheim

Made in the USA
Columbia, SC
01 June 2018